Nobody Was Here

7th Grade in the Life of Me, Penelope

Nobody Was Here

7th Grade in the Life of Me, Penelope

ALISON POLLET

SCHOLASTIC INC.

New York Toronto London Auckland Sydney
Mexico City New Delhi Hong Kong Buenos Aires

ISBN 0-439-58395-0

Excerpt from *Charlotte's Web* on page 214 copyright © 1952 by E. B. White, renewed © 1980 by E. B. White. Used by permission of HarperCollins Publishers. "Everyday I Write the Book" by Elvis Costello © 1983 BMG Music Publishing Ltd. (PRS). All rights for the U.S. obo BMG Music Publishing Ltd. (PRS) administered by BMG Songs, Inc. (ASCAP). "The Greatest Thing" by Elvis Costello © 1983 BMG Music Publishing Ltd. (PRS). All rights for the U.S. obo BMG Music Publishing Ltd. (PRS) administered by BMG Songs, Inc. (ASCAP).

12 11 10 9 8 7 6 5 4 3 2   5 6 7 8 9 10/0

Printed in the U.S.A.   40

First paperback printing, January 2005

Original hardcover edition designed by Marijka Kostiw, published by Orchard Books, an imprint of Scholastic Inc., July 2004

Text type set in 11-point Hoefler Text
Display type set in Circus Dog

M. P.,
S. P.,
and
J. P.,

*Thank You
for Everything*

Part one

ELSTON ELEMENTARY SCHOOL

6TH GRADE FINAL REPORT CARD
SPRING, 1981

NAME: Penelope B. Schwartzbaum

FINAL GRADES:

ENGLISH: A
SOCIAL STUDIES: B+
MATH: B-
SCIENCE: B-
ART: A-
MUSIC: B+
GYM: Pass

REMARKS: Perfectly intelligent but has tendency to drift off during class periods. Will do fine in middle school as long as inattention does not worsen. Is timely, polite, and rarely impudent. Has irritating habit of altering penmanship style on monthly basis. (Perhaps an identity issue — guidance counselor would do well to take note.)

Chapter One

"Hey, weirdo, wake up! We're almost there."

"Yooooooo hooooooooo . . ."

"Earth to Penelope!"

Penelope Schwartzbaum felt like her brain was rattling inside her head. She'd fallen asleep on the jostling school bus, her head against the window, using a spiral notebook as a pillow. She untangled the spiral from her hair, rubbed her eyes, and slowly twisted her neck to the left. A giant red face glowered at her.

As twelve-year-olds go, Penelope's best friend, Stacy Commack, was on the small side. But she was one of those people who, by sheer force of personality, appeared much larger than she actually was. Stacy had spent the summer at her father's beach house in California, and underneath her dirty-blond curls her dimpled, sunburned face resembled a peeling red potato.

Stacy was an impatient sort, and today she was particularly twitchy. "How can you sleep at a time like this?" she shouted at Penelope, flakes of sunburned skin flying off her nose. "It's the first day of middle school, we don't have any classes together, we're not even in the same homeroom. Half the kids in our grade are going to be new. Everything's different!"

"Sorry," yawned Penelope, who had a tendency to apologize when it wasn't necessary. *I haven't really been sleeping,* she thought defensively, *I've just been resting — with my eyes closed.* She didn't bother to explain that to Stacy, who was simultaneously memorizing her class schedule and reorganizing her pencil case. Penelope made sure her eyes stayed open the rest of the ride.

The bus took a sharp left off the expressway onto a leafy, tree-lined street. Soon its giant wheels were crunching the circular gravel driveway of Elston Preparatory School. It lurched to a stop, and kids tumbled toward the door, a colorful chain of satin jackets and backpacks, like plastic toy monkeys falling out of their barrel, still interlinked. Stacy flung herself into the line, dragging Penelope with her. The first period of the first day of school was minutes away. "Hurry up!" she yowled. "We can't be late."

Penelope just wished she could go back to sleep.

But minutes later, she was propped in a wooden desk chair beneath a hot fluorescent light, listening to her homeroom teacher, Dr. Alvin, deliver a "Welcome, seventh graders, to the middle and upper school campus" speech. A pointy-faced woman wearing a Milk Duds–brown sweater rolled up to her elbows, Dr. Alvin leaned over her desk and peered into the rainbow sea of brand-new, not-yet-washed polo shirts. She coughed:

"Aah-heh-aah-hem," and waited until the room was silent of rustling papers and uncapping pen tops.

"Ladies and gentlemen, I'm going to tell you this now, before the school year really starts. I'm going to tell you this now, so that when things get tough you can't say you weren't warned: This year we're going to try and break you." Dr. Alvin's lips smacked on the word "you," and Penelope, a skinny girl with freckles across her nose and brown hair that hung flat against her cheeks, felt as if she were already breaking, snapping in half like one of the Number 2 pencils in the front pouch of her backpack.

"We might try and break you, but you don't have to let us. You can work hard. You can persevere. Do so and you'll be rewarded. If you succeed at Elston Prep, you'll go anywhere you want." The class erupted in a deep collective sigh, the kind actors in soda commercials make after a super-refreshing sip: *Ahhhhhh*. They knew what Dr. Alvin meant by "anywhere you want." *College. Any college you want.* Getting into a good college was the whole point of Elston Prep.

In the margins of her notebook Penelope scribbled: *Getting into a good college is the whole point of life.*

She crossed out the words until they were obliterated by an inky smudge the size of a thumb.

"We're all aware what 'prep' in 'Elston Prep' stands for, right? Preparatory. Meaning we're preparing you. And not only for higher education, but for a fulfilling life of the mind. Homework will be extreme. We're talking five, six hours a night. You're going to need to be disciplined. What you learn in seventh grade will be a foundation for what you learn in eighth and then in high school. What you learn now will help you later. But what you don't learn now will hurt you later."

To signal that this part of the speech was over, Dr. Alvin sank into a swively chair behind her desk. The class stared nervously as she flipped open her roll book, as if perhaps their seventh-grade fates were already written inside. But the teacher simply moved onto what she called the nuts and bolts of homeroom: roll call, locker assignments, tardiness, and absences.

A breeze snuck in through a cracked-open window, and Penelope placed her hand on her notebook to stop the pages from fluttering. She looked at the notes she'd taken during Dr. Alvin's lecture:

Pay attention.
We're going to try and break you.
Homework: 6 hours a night.
Don't get behind.
Catching up is very difficult.

Penelope used a thick purple pen. In her neat, loopy writing, the words didn't look as scary as they'd sounded coming out of Dr. Alvin's mouth. They looked bubbly and nice, and for a second she forgot to be petrified.

♥ ♥ ♥ ♥ ♥

In seventh grade there was nothing more important than having a best friend, and Penelope had never been more aware of this than today. If it hadn't been for Stacy, she wouldn't have made it through the first day. In fact, if it hadn't been for Stacy, she wouldn't have made it to Algebra class.

Elston Preparatory School was special for a New York City school: A forty-five-minute drive from Manhattan, it boasted three separate campuses — one for nursery, one for elementary, and another for middle and high school students. The middle and high school campus, though only a block away from the elementary one, was twice the size. With its lush green fields and looming buildings, its libraries, laboratories, and gymnasiums, it was a giant new world for seventh graders like Penelope and Stacy.

"Guess who's in my homeroom," announced Stacy as she and Penelope trotted across campus, their brand-new white Tretorns — saved just for today — falling easily into step. They had half the day and lunch behind them; afternoon classes were about to begin. "Anabella Blumberg. Isn't that weird?"

"Mmmmm hmmmmm," agreed Penelope.

"She looks really good. Hey, what do you have now? You have Algebra, right? With Mr. Bobkin? I had that second period. I'm just warning you, he's scary."

As easily as Penelope and Stacy had fallen into

step, they fell out, as Penelope — who was having trouble navigating the maze of cobblestone pathways that connected Elston's buildings — took an unintentional turn to the right. "Hey, you're going the wrong way!" Stacy shouted, grabbing her friend's elbow. "No offense, Penelope, but you have to pay attention."

But Penelope *was* paying attention — just to all the wrong things. How could she concentrate on navigating the campus when being here was like visiting the Museum of Natural History? Except the exhibits had come to life!

A tall girl in a shredded Elston High School sweatshirt, wrists full of silver bangles, clanged past.

A boy in a Harvard sweatshirt yelled, "Friedman, catch!" then hurled a Nerf football into the air.

An eighth-grade girl bent down to tie the rainbow heart shoelaces on her red-and-white Nikes.

And here were girls from their grade: Lillian Lang and Annie Reed carried bulging Le Sportsac bags over their shoulders — the bags were so heavy, their wiry bodies sloped toward each other like bent paper clips. Pia Smith and Annabella Blumberg passed, laughing and pointing as they walked, at what Penelope wasn't sure. Vicki Feld and Tillie Warner studied a notebook as they shuffled past.

The seventh grade was like Noah's Ark, divided into sets of two, and now that they were on a new campus — surrounded by new buildings and new classmates — the pairs clung to each other even tighter. So if there were things about Stacy that bothered Penelope, she did her best to ignore them. Because if she thought about those things, she might get mad, and then she'd have to think about *not* being best friends with Stacy. And when you've been best friends as long as Penelope and Stacy had — since they were six! six years! half their lives! — *not being best friends* was something you didn't think about. Thinking about that was even more disorienting than getting lost on campus. It was like listening to your voice on a tape recorder, or getting eyedrops in your eyes, or waking up one morning to find out that the world is tilted.

When they arrived at Penelope's Algebra class in Gritzfield Hall, she had no idea how they'd gotten there. It had been too easy to not look where she was going, and to let Stacy lead.

Chapter Two

Sometimes ignoring could be a lot of work.

Penelope and Stacy emerged from Williams Bar-Be-Cue onto the corner of Eighty-sixth and Broadway, where Stacy stopped dead in her tracks, scrunched up her nose, and hissed, "Peee-ewwwww!" She tossed a grease-spotted paper bag of fried chicken at Penelope, who caught it just in time.

Blocks later, on Eighty-first Street, Stacy was still pinching her nose with exaggerated force. "I guess I'm just getting more sensitive to bad smells," she said when she finally felt safe to unclamp her nostrils. "My stepmother says that's what happens when women mature — odors bother them." Penelope had never heard that. She *had* noticed that lately Stacy had been scrunching her nose up all over the neighborhood. Places she'd gone her whole life, too: Williams, Broadway Nut Shop, Burger Joint.

Most kids who went to Elston Elementary lived on New York City's Upper East Side, so living across the park on the Upper West Side was a point of pride for Penelope and Stacy. "West is best!" they'd happily shouted when Elston Elementary's lone West Side school bus parted ways on the expressway with the fleet of East Side ones. "East is least!"

But that had been sixth grade. *Now* here was Stacy complaining that Broadway, the street she and her mother lived on, was a giant stink bomb. "Oh, please!" Stacy's mother scoffed when Stacy brought up the subject of moving across town. Shirley Commack was a reporter for the *New York Times* who cursed a lot and liked to talk about the good old days when she was a hippie at war protests. She wouldn't be caught dead on the pristine Upper East Side, and dreaded the thought that the West Side could get fancy like that. "You think Broadway stinks?" she argued. "Park Avenue is what stinks. Of boredom!"

Stacy and Shirley Commack lived in a building that looked more like a fortress than an apartment building, with its black gated courtyard, tiers, and towers. When Stacy and Penelope had been little, they'd pretended it was a castle: They were princesses; the doormen were palace guards; the elevator operators, knights; and Bernice, the Commacks' housekeeper, a fiery dragon entrusted to protect them.

After delivering the chicken to Stacy's mother, who often had cravings for takeout when staying up all night on deadline, Penelope and Stacy retreated to Stacy's bedroom. Her father had paid to have it redone, and Stacy had been allowed to pick the theme, which was rainbows.

There were rainbow sheets, a matching quilt and curtains, and satin pillows in the shape of rainbows;

there was a new desk; a new full-length mirror; and a new bookcase, empty except for Judy Blume's *Forever* and *Wifey,* since any book marked "Ages 8 to 12" had been boxed and shipped to Stacy's nine-year-old step-sister in California.

"Do you think I should wear a pink or yellow oxford with these? If I wear the yellow, I can wear my white Nikes with the yellow swooshes. I was saving those for the second week, but I guess it's okay." Stacy was standing before her open closet, one of her mother's slender reporter's notebooks in one hand, a pair of white Levi's in the other. She consulted the notebook: "I guess I'll save them for next week and wear my penny loafers tomorrow. Did you see how Tillie Warner wore French coins in hers? I think that's tacky. So, do you want to plan your outfit? If you ask me, you should wear your painter's pants. Not the white ones, the red ones. And don't wear that orange Lacoste with the red painter's pants like that one time. They don't match."

It had been a long first day, and a thought buzzed into Penelope's tired brain: *We don't match.* In the six years she'd been best friends with Stacy, she'd never had a thought like that. It was shocking! She tried swatting it away like a mosquito. *Think of anything else!* she told herself. *Think of a song! Think about* General Hospital*!* She stared hard at her feet, as if concentrating on her white sneakers — they were gleaming against

Stacy's plush new grape-colored carpet — would hypnotize her into forgetting the bad thought.

"Remember you swore you weren't going to wear the white jeans tomorrow," Stacy reminded Penelope as she was getting on the elevator. Penelope didn't remember swearing anything, but she nodded agreeably as the elevator doors inched shut, leaving her on one side and Stacy on the other.

How funny it could be, running into someone you knew on the street. Sometimes the people most familiar to you were the least recognizable when you saw them in an unexpected place.

It took Penelope a few seconds to realize that the lanky woman in a pin-striped suit in front of Red Apple Supermarket was none other than her mother, Denise Schwartzbaum. She had her brown leather briefcase gripped tightly between her feet, leaving her hands free to rummage in a bin of yellow potatoes.

Not only was Denise Schwartzbaum unfazed by the sudden presence of Penelope, she acted as if her daughter had been by her side all along — like they'd come to the grocery store together and Penelope had just run to Aisle 4 to get the cream cheese.

"Hi, Mom," greeted Penelope.

"I'm so tired," responded her mother.

If people could have slogans, Penelope figured "I'm

so tired" would be her mother's. She used it instead of "hellos" and "good nights," or as an answer to the question "How was your day?" (If she said: "I'm so tired," it meant "not so good.")

"There are too many kinds of potatoes," complained Mrs. Schwartzbaum, holding a waxy yellow one in her left palm while eyeing a bin of brown Idahos. "It's oppressive."

Penelope asked what she meant.

"Overwhelming," she answered, dropping the potato into the bin with a thud. "Life was easier when there were two kinds of potatoes: regular and sweet." She let out a long, exasperated sigh. "And all these onions . . . pearl onions, Vidalia onions, yellow, red, white, Spanish . . . blah, blah, blah."

A loudspeaker announced a sale on spinach pasta, and a gray-haired lady in an I ♥ NY sweatshirt careened past them, accidentally stabbing Penelope's mother's ankle with the spoke jutting from her metal shopping cart.

"That's the last straw," heaved Mrs. Schwartzbaum, watching the tiny hole in her stockings fast becoming a run. "I was going to make dinner. Chicken and potatoes like your father likes, but I had a vicious day at the office. Sometimes you just have to admit you can't do everything. I'm too tired to cook. How does Italian takeout sound to you?"

They headed to Al Buon Gusto to get take-out

spaghetti with meatballs for four with extra garlic bread on the side.

The Schwartzbaum family lived in a stout gray apartment building with a dark green awning that took up a block of West End Avenue. Inside was a lobby that resembled a ballroom in a Disney movie, with shimmering marble floors, mirrored chandeliers, and dark muraled walls.

Penthouse C on the sixteenth floor was known to New Yorkers as a "classic seven," which meant it had a kitchen, a living room, a dining room, a maid's room that Penelope's father, Herbert Schwartzbaum, had remodeled as an office, and three bedrooms — one for Penelope, one for her parents, and another for her little brother, Nathaniel. The living room had big windows that opened like gates onto West End Avenue, and from the tiny windows in Penelope's room, you could look over the tops of buildings toward the green stretch of Riverside Park.

That night, as the cars hummed down West End Avenue, with Dr. Alvin's warnings ringing in her ears, Penelope bent over the yellow corner desk and did the first day's assignments in a state of deliberate concentration. For each assignment, she wrote a rough draft, which she copied over in her neatest, most careful handwriting.

Oh, Penelope loved writing! Not *writing* writing as

in writing stories or poems. She loved *writing*. Period. Penelope loved to study people's handwriting, to try to imitate the curves of their Cs and the crosses of their Ts. So when she was done with her homework, she gave herself a little reward. She spread all of her new notebooks and textbooks out on the desk, opening each one to the first page. In the top right-hand corner she wrote her name. At first she was careful to use the exact same writing:

Penelope B. Schwartzbaum
Penelope B. Schwartzbaum
Penelope B. Schwartzbaum

By the time she got to her Earth Science textbook, she was bored. She started experimenting. She did bubble letters:

Penelope B. Schwartzbaum

She slanted her letters to the right.

Penelope B. Schwartzbaum

She did all lowercase.

penelope b. schwartzbaum

All caps.

PENELOPE B. SCHWARTZBAUM

She did script.

Penelope B. Schwartzbaum

♥ ♥ ♥ ♥ ♥

All the millions of ways one could tilt one's pen, all the trillions of ways one could puff one's Ps, loop one's Ls: It filled Penelope up — as if the world were bigger than she could ever imagine. Bigger than Stacy and Dr. Alvin, bigger than the Upper East Side and Upper West Side combined. Her pen did its orderly dance across the page, and the world felt calm like the Hudson River on a dark, warm night.

A Quiz for Penelope B. Schwartzbaum

Prepared by Penelope B. Schwartzbaum

Name: Penelope B. Schwartzbaum

Age: 12

Grade: 7th

Color of Hair: Brown

Color of Eyes: Green

Height: 5' 2"

Weight: Don't have a scale!

Favorite Food: Pizza

Least Favorite Food: Marzipan (Don't try it. It's
    gross.)

Favorite Outfit: Anything Polo, and everything
    should match.

Best Friend: Stacy Commack (Of course!)

Are Your Parents Married, Divorced, or
    Separated? (Underline one.)

Favorite Television Show: General Hospital (Of
    course, again!)

To be continued . . .

Chapter Three

Pia Smith sent a clipboard skidding like an air hockey puck across the table. She was a pie-faced girl with a wide space between her eyes, frizzy hair pulled back with shiny purple combs, and a bad habit of saying every sentence like a question. "Sign this?" she ordered, plopping across from Stacy and Penelope.

Penelope dunked a chicken finger into a glob of ketchup. "What is it?" Stacy asked.

"It's The Pledge. Just sign it, will you?"

Penelope and Stacy read from the ruled paper snapped to the clipboard:

THE PLEDGE

I WENT TO ELSTON ELEMENTARY SCHOOL.

I PLEDGE NOT TO BECOME FRIENDS WITH ANY NEW KIDS.

THAT MEANS I WILL NOT GO OVER TO THE HOUSE OF or ATTEND PARTIES OF or TALK (MORE THAN ABSOLUTELY NECESSARY) TO KIDS WHO JUST STARTED ELSTON.

"What's the problem with the new kids?" Stacy sounded purposeful, like an interviewer on *60 Minutes,* a tactic she'd picked up from her mother.

"They're all abnormal," answered Pia, reaching across the table to snatch a chicken finger off Penelope's plate. She had half of it in her mouth when she thought to ask, "Mind if I have one?" Pia was always dieting but could often be found eating off other people's plates. "We're getting T-shirts that say NO NEWKS. You know, spelled: N-E-W-K-S? Like 'NO NUKES'? As in 'NO NUCLEAR WAR'? If you sign now, you'll definitely get one. They're going to be cute *and* for a good cause. I'm telling you, new kids suck."

Pia spat the last angry sentence, then looked around proudly as if she hoped a new kid had heard her. But they were too far away. While the Elston Elementary alumni ate lunch in the center of the cafeteria, the new kids dined at the tables on the outskirts — like tiny islands surrounding a dark, impenetrable sea.

"Trust me," insisted Pia. "I've talked to a bunch of them. They're rude, and anyway, it's the principle of the thing. Ever heard of loyalty? We should stick together."

Stacy inspected the clipboard with deliberation. "Who wrote this?" she asked, even though she knew it had been Annabella Blumberg. Annabella had been the brains behind last year's very successful Roll Up Your Left Pant Leg If You Hate Hallie Alterman Day and the equally effective Put a Sticker on Your Notebook If You Think Richie Chernovsky Smells Day, and this was just the kind of thing she would organize — or have someone else organize.

22

That someone else was *always* Pia.

Pia was Annabella's best friend, her assistant in command, her head negotiator in chief, and her fiercest protector. She was scariest when she was around Annabella. Alone, she was easier to say no to. Or at least maybe.

"We need to think about it," Stacy said plainly.

"What?" Pia sounded dumbfounded.

"Penelope and I, *we* need to think about it." As the words left Stacy's mouth again, time seemed to slow down so that Penelope could actually see Pia's face go from pink to magenta to scarlet.

"Penelope and I, we need to think about it." Penelope heard the words again in her head.

A disgusted Pia nabbed the clipboard from Stacy, turned on her heels as if to leave, then turned back to grab Penelope's last chicken finger. "I bet if Annabella had asked, then you would have signed," she grumbled before thumping off in a huff.

"Wow," whistled Stacy, taking a sip of her Pepsi Light.

On any other day, Penelope might have relished the moments after a scene like that — rarely did life flare up so dramatically, and in her presence. But today, all she could think was: *"We* need to think about it." *Not I need to think about it. We! Are we a "we"? Do I want to sign something? Do I want to make a pledge?*

"What's wrong with you?" asked Stacy. "You look weird. Like you have something to say."

Penelope opened her mouth to talk, but her thoughts were going too fast for her mouth. She thought: *We're not a we. We don't match.* She hadn't planned on saying the words out loud, but they tumbled from her lips like static-y socks flying out of an open dryer.

"We'renotawe. Wedon'tmatch."

Had the words left her mouth? They had! She hadn't meant for them to! Penelope's hand flew in front of her mouth, as if she could physically stop any more stupid words from coming out. Two tables over, a pyramid of soda cans crashed with a giant clang.

"Huh?" said Stacy. "What'd you say?"

Penelope scrambled to recover. She steered her thoughts to Port Charles, home of her favorite television show, *General Hospital*. "I *said* I was thinking about Rick and Monica," she lied. Rick and Monica — or Dr. Weber and Dr. Quartermaine, as they were also known — were characters who were having a dangerous and passionate affair.

"Oh," said Stacy, as if that made perfect sense.

Vicki Feld and Tillie Warner arrived at the table. "Is Pia Smith pathetic or what?" groused Vicki, sliding into Pia's abandoned chair. "Pathetic" and "pitiful" were the seventh grade's most popular words. They were "in," like ballet slippers, Lacoste sweaters, and friendship pins.

"Yeah, she's so scared Annabella's not gonna be most popular this year, it's pitiful," said Tillie.

Vicki was the kind of girl other girls called "cute" and not only because she was exceptionally short. She looked permanently animated — and not animated as in *lively*. Vicki looked like a cartoon character. With hair more yellow than blond, as if it had been colored with a crayon, a mouth of white Chiclet teeth, and chubby, pinchable cheeks, she was a cross between Betty from Archie Comics and Smurfette — if Smurfette weren't blue.

Vicki's best friend, Tillie, didn't look like anyone you'd see on TV — unless it was a commercial for cortisone cream or hair conditioner. A rashy girl who picked at her split ends and rarely looked at you when she talked, Tillie wore a sleeveless pink polo that exposed pale white arms dotted with red bumps — an allergic reaction, she claimed, to the lab coats they wore for Earth Science.

"So then you're not going to sign The Pledge?" Stacy asked them.

Vicki liked to act like everything that came out of her mouth was top secret. And while she often whispered, she had a habit of whispering *loudly*. "Oh, we will," she rasped.

Knowing what she'd said required explanation, Vicki did a careful scan of the cafeteria to make sure the coast was clear. When she was sure no one else was listening, she slowly mouthed the words "Annabella's bat mitzvah . . ." She gave a deep and knowing nod of the head, as if that said it all. "It's sorta blackmail," she added, "but I heard she's getting a glassblower *and* a deejay."

Tillie focused on the table when she talked. "I think it's funny that Annabella and Pia think you can control who you like," she told the crumbly remains of Stacy's oatmeal cookie. "Like, if I want to be friends with a new kid, I'm not going to let myself?"

"You're so philosophical," scoffed Vicki. "You know you wanna go to Annabella's bat mitzvah. You already talked about the dress you'd buy."

Stacy jumped in. "I agree you wouldn't want someone to *tell* you who to be friends with, but what if, well . . ." Stacy seemed to be thinking out loud. "What if you just happened to never get to know them?" Her eyes darted toward the new kids' tables off to the side. "Then it wouldn't be a problem."

Tillie squinted at the packets of salt and pepper.

"It's up to you!" Stacy added triumphantly — as if she'd just succeeded in decoding her own muddled thoughts. "You don't have to like anyone you don't want to!" Stacy's final sentence sounded to Penelope like a warped version of a public service announcement about peer pressure they showed on Channel 11 in between sitcom reruns.

"I predict that Annabella's bat mitzvah will be the party of the year," announced Vicki conspiratorially. "There will be all these cute boys there. She has all these camp friends, you know." Vicki looked directly at Tillie. "You can't pretend you don't care about that. I mean, we're in seventh grade. We all want boyfriends."

We do? thought Penelope, who looked from Vicki grinning commandingly to Stacy nodding agreeably to Tillie painstakingly dividing a strand of hair into two silky threads. She had the sudden flash that perhaps there were thoughts inside Tillie's head that no one, even Vicki, knew.

Algebra was Penelope's worst subject. The teacher, Mr. Bobkin, was a balding man with a beard, and a belly so large, it seemed to Penelope it had a personality all its own. Like it was pacing the room and Mr. Bobkin was chasing it. Some teachers wore jeans and a sweater. Not Mr. Bobkin. He wore a suit and tie — the same tie, actually — every day. It was silk and red and dotted with gold "Es" in honor of the institution that reared him. "That's right, kids," he'd told the horrified class, their eyes bulging like the giant green olives Penelope's mother served at cocktail parties. "Once upon a time I was you."

The only time the stern man cracked a smile was when he recalled his days as a seventh grader at Elston. Back then, the school was all boys, they had to wear uniforms, and they treated their elders with respect. He didn't say "as opposed to now," but Penelope knew that's what he meant. She also suspected he liked Elston better back then because girls hadn't been allowed.

Still, Penelope would rather hear Bobkin's recollections of Elston past than his lectures on Algebra. The teacher talked so fast and didn't take questions until the end of the period, at which point Penelope was totally lost. It would happen suddenly, the getting lost, so suddenly that — when looking back at it — she couldn't recall the exact moment it happened.

Like today. She was sitting at her desk, hunched over her notebook, taking notes, when — boom! — the letters and numbers were crashing and jamming in her head, and she stopped taking notes and started practicing her signature in the margins of the pages. Over and over and over again:

Penelope B. Schwartzbaum
Penelope B. Schwartzbaum
Penelope B. Schwartzbaum

She studied the carvings on the wood desk. She didn't know who any of the initials belonged to. Probably they were the older kids she saw in the halls. **L.K. = #1 SHOOTING GUARD. H.S. AND A.H. = PRETTIEST JUNIORS. M.M. AND L.A. FRIENDS 4 LIFE!** It was like *General Hospital*. Maybe some of them were even having affairs! Like Rick and Monica!

A.G. ♥'S K.B. N.L. AND D.K. 2GETHER4EVER!
K.A. L–U–VS R.D.!

She went back to practicing her signature.

A curly-haired boy next to her slammed his textbook shut, and Penelope snapped out of her daze to discover that class was over. "That sucks, huh?" muttered the boy, who also happened to be a new kid. He wore a retainer that clicked when he talked.

"Yeah," agreed Penelope, though she didn't know exactly *what* sucked.

"A quiz tomorrow with no notice! I have to read Act I of *Julius Caesar*. When am I gonna study for this? I'm Ben," he said in a rush of clicks and words.

"Penelope," she said.

"Me Ben, you Pen," grinned the boy.

They packed up their backpacks and exited the classroom.

Gym was the only class the entire seventh grade had together. Bobkin let them out late, and the Algebra class swarmed like bees toward the gymnasium. "He does this on purpose," gulped Ben as they jogged across campus. "He's such a jerk. I'm glad I didn't go to Elston when he was there. Bunch of nerds in suits."

"Yeah, well, I wouldn't have been allowed," puffed Penelope.

"Huh?" said Ben.

"No girls," she reminded him.

"Well, then, I'm double glad I didn't go to Elston back then," clicked Ben, giving Penelope a sideways glance. "I like going to school with girls."

Penelope heard Vicki Feld's voice — *we all want boyfriends* — in her head and ran just a little bit faster.

Chapter Four

It always happened this way. Right before the school year started, Penelope's mother set lofty goals for herself: *This year, no matter how much stress she was under, she was going to come home every night at 6 P.M. This year, she was going to make home-cooked meals for her children. This year, she wasn't doing any overtime. No dinner meetings. No business travel. She was going to set limits.* Then, a week or so later — after five nights in a row of ordering takeout and paying the housekeeper overtime because she was running late — Mrs. Schwartzbaum gave up and hired someone to help out.

This came up that night at the dinner table after Penelope's father excused himself to pack for a business trip and Penelope's brother, Nathaniel, scampered off to watch television. Penelope and her mother were still picking at their dinner: take-out spaghetti and meatballs — again.

"Hey, Mom, where'd you go to college?" asked Penelope. Along with Annabella's bat mitzvah and how much homework they had, college was the most popular subject in the seventh grade.

"I went to City College. Same with your dad. We had to live at home because our parents didn't have any money. You're lucky. You'll be able to go wherever you want."

"That's what Dr. Alvin says." Penelope twirled spaghetti onto her fork. "If we do well."

"You'll do well," replied her mother matter-of-factly. As vice president of client relations for one of New York City's most prominent financial conglomerates, Denise Schwartzbaum took it for granted that her daughter was bound for great things. "So, this is showing some gumption. You're thinking about college already?"

"Stacy thinks we need to pick."

"That Stacy," marveled Mrs. Schwartzbaum. "Always on top of things." Her mother paused to spool spaghetti onto her fork. "I know a real expert on college you can talk to," she told Penelope in a tone that was almost teasing.

Penelope stared at her mother. "Who?" she asked.

"Jenny. She's the new mother's helper I hired."

Penelope felt like she'd swallowed the meatball whole. She stared at her plate. There was no spaghetti left, only clumps of meat in oily orange puddles.

As her fork scraped white stripes into the orange splats on her plate, she thought about the Lacoste shirt she'd wear tomorrow — white with red stripes — and whether she should wear it with jeans or corduroys.

"Jenny would be an excellent person to talk to

about college. She goes to Columbia. That's an Ivy League school, you know."

Should I wear a belt, and if so, which one? The ribbon one with the alligators, or the rainbow one? And should I wear red Polo socks or tube socks or . . .

"She starts work here tomorrow. I gotta say, it's a huge relief for me."

Sneakers or loafers? If sneakers, then tube socks. If loafers, then red Polo socks.

"I've got three reports to write in two months, and your father, you know how busy he is. This month alone he's got trips to Paris, Copenhagen, and Singapore. So, it's a good thing, eh?"

You know what would look really cool with the red and white shirt? Those little red earrings they had at Bloomingdale's.

"Honey, are you listening to anything I'm saying?"

If only my ears hadn't closed up . . .

"I know you're twelve and you think that's too old for a babysitter."

What a funny expression! Ears closing up!

"I think it would help if you thought of her as Nathaniel's babysitter. And call her a mother's helper, why don't you? I think that will make it easier for you. Okay?"

Penelope pinched her earlobes, squeezing the hard little lumps that used to be holes.

"Okay?"

She squeezed tighter until the lumps felt hot between her fingers.

"Listen, you know your dad and I would like to be home more. We'd like that more than anything, but we just can't be. . . . I tried. I really did. Jenny will be a great help to you if you just let her. Be a trooper, okay? For me?"

Ouch!

"Okay? Please, Penelope, say something. I'm counting on you to be mature here."

Penelope knew she was supposed to say something reassuring, like: "Of course I'll be a trooper. Don't worry, Mom, I'll be nice to Jenny." But, the words that came out were: "Can we go shopping for school clothes?"

Her mother sighed and said she'd see when she was free.

The next day, Penelope got off the school bus, but didn't enter her building. Instead, she waited on the sidewalk outside the apartment for her brother to arrive. A game she and Stacy played as kids, Mother May I, was going through her head. Only it came out in an unexpected way:

Mother's Helper, may I take a giant step?

Penelope knew from experience that the first days with a new mother's helper were pretty uncomfortable.

Mother's Helper, may I take a medium step?

She wondered if Jenny knew this.

Mother's Helper, may I take a baby step?

Probably not! Probably Jenny had never even been a mother's helper!

Penelope didn't realize she was actually taking the steps. Had there been anyone looking at her from across the street, she might have looked like she was performing a particularly clunky modern dance number. She was mid–giant step when the elementary school bus inched to the corner, and Nathaniel disembarked, a scruffy eight-year-old in a satin baseball jacket and jeans that wrinkled at the knees.

"Hey, Penelope!"

Penelope fished inside her front pocket for a quarter. "Heads we go to Baronet and play videos, tails we go upstairs!" she responded.

"But Mom said we had to go *straight* home," the boy warned.

"So? It's not like Jenny is gonna know we went to Baronet. We can just tell her we get out at four-thirty on Tuesdays." Penelope grabbed Nathaniel's skinny wrist and inspected his Mickey Mouse watch. It was 4:01. "See? We have twenty-nine minutes."

Nathaniel shuffled from foot to foot. "I gotta go to the bathroom!"

"Baronet has a bathroom."

"It's yucky."

Penelope was already in a rotten mood, and her whining little brother was making it worse. He had a knack for doing that.

"Maybe she's looking down at us right now?" Nathaniel tilted his head up to their apartment on the sixteenth floor. "Like how Ivy used to do. . . ." His voice got softer when he said the name "Ivy." She'd been their mother's helper for two years until she moved to California to attend graduate school, and if Penelope and Nathaniel agreed on anything, it was that they'd loved her very much.

"Yeah, well, she's not Ivy. She's not gonna know to do that. And anyway, she doesn't know what we look like."

Nathaniel's shoulders slumped in defeat. "Fine, flip a coin," he said. They squatted on the sidewalk, their backpacks by their sides. Penelope placed the quarter on her thumb and flicked it in the air. It did a triple somersault and landed with a *plink* on the cement: tails.

"Two outta three!" she yelped, grabbing the quarter to flip it again.

But Nathaniel stood up and walked toward the apartment. "Hey!" Penelope called, running to grab a satin elbow. She put on her sweetest voice and patted his dirty-blond head. "C'mon, Natty, pretty please! I'll buy you a game of Asteroids."

"Tails we go upstairs. You said. And, Pen, I really gotta go!"

"I'll get you a Charleston Chew!" Penelope cooed. "They have strawberry there, just like you like."

Nathaniel kept walking.

"Fine." Penelope marched ahead of him. "Have it your way."

Inside the lobby, the building's doorman Carlos was using a rag, the same dark shade of green as his cap, to shine the wooden panel between elevators. "*Hola,* young Penelope and young Nathaniel."

"*Hola,*" said Penelope and Nathaniel in unison.

Carlos beamed. He saw it as his personal mission to teach the kids in the building introductory Spanish. "So, the new lady's upstairs," he whispered conspiratorially.

"Yeah," said Penelope, "we know."

"Boy, do I feel sorry for you two. . . ." Carlos's deep voice oozed with pity.

"What do you mean?" whispered Nathaniel, his body stiffening with fright.

"Well . . . ," said Carlos, crinkling his nose like he smelled garbage. "Let's just say you'll see for yourself."

Penelope's own stomach began to churn fearfully, until she remembered: Not only was Carlos the resident language instructor, he was also the building's most artful storyteller. "He's lying, dummy," she blurted out, punching her brother's bony shoulder.

"You're getting too smart for your own good, Penelope!" Carlos said, laughing. He turned to Nathaniel.

"Don't worry, kiddo. She looks super nice. Maybe even as nice as the last one, and you know how I felt about her." Carlos stopped wiping the counter to thump his wide chest with his hand. He'd loved Ivy as much as they had, and thumping his chest meant she had his heart.

The elevator doors heaved open to reveal the amber walls of the sixteenth floor, and with a quick turn of the head Penelope got her first glimpse of Jenny leaning in the doorway of the apartment. She smashed her eyelids shut and imagined that when she opened her eyes, Jenny wouldn't be there. A gym teacher's voice in her head yelled, *Go back, go back!* She wanted Jenny to backpedal like an outfielder going for a fly ball deep in center field. Except she'd just keep going back and back and back . . . until she disappeared. Poof! Gone!

Penelope walked blindly down the familiar hallway. *Mother's Helper, may I take a baby step? Another baby step? You didn't say, 'Mother's Helper, may I'!*

She cracked open her lids.

Was she gone?

No. She was there. Live, in color, and she smelled like the inside of an orange peel. "Are you Jenny?" swooned Nathaniel.

Penelope and Nathaniel hung their jackets on pegs in the front hall closet. "You guys want a snack?" Jenny asked.

"I'm hungry!" boomed Nathaniel as if this weren't a boring answer to a boring question, but a big bright idea that had come to him from nowhere. "I'll take a snack!"

"I thought you had to go to the bathroom so badly," Penelope muttered to her brother. "Liar," she whispered so only he could hear it.

Nathaniel shoved past Penelope and scurried down the hallway, limbs flying. "Oooh, I forgot!" he howled.

Of all the mother's helpers the Schwartzbaums had ever employed, Jenny was definitely the prettiest. She had thick blond hair, glowy pink cheeks, and fluttery white eyelashes that made her green eyes twinkle when she blinked. In her stretched white sweatshirt worn inside out over the most faded Levi's jeans Penelope had ever seen, Jenny gave an overall appearance of softness.

She seems nice, better than I had expected. Maybe she'll be like Ivy. Maybe Jenny will make Carlos thump his chest. Nathaniel will love her, I will love her . . . and then . . .

Penelope shook her head from side to side, as if doing so would erase the thoughts inside it. Staring at the nice, pretty face, she had the sudden urge to get as far away from it as possible. "I forgot I have to go pick up some school supplies at Baronet," she gulped. She ran into the kitchen and called Stacy. Then, her jacket was back on and she was in the elevator going down.

Chapter Five

As a kid growing up in New York City, Penelope knew lots of ways to make walking down the street interesting.

Don't step on a crack or you'll break your mother's back.

Don't step on a line or you'll hurt your father's spine.

But scanning the streets for Moe Was Heres was her favorite. Moe was the Upper West Side's most notorious graffiti artist. He scratched his name into phone booths, spray-painted it on subway cars, etched it in the sidewalk. Penelope had counted twenty-two Moe Was Heres on West End Avenue and Broadway between Ninetieth and Seventy-seventh streets alone. Finding new Moe Was Heres was a competition for kids on the Upper West Side. Like an Easter egg hunt, only every day and slightly more sinister. After all, what Moe did was graffiti. Which was illegal! Very illegal! There were always stories on the news about it and signs on lampposts and phone booths with warnings about how graffiti was a crime.

So, as Penelope walked the ten blocks from her house to Baronet, she kept her head hanging down and her eyes peeled. On the corner of Eighty-sixth Street, there were the fading chalky remains of a hopscotch game; in between Eighty-fourth and Eighty-fifth, there was a train of pink silly string; Eighty-second was covered in litter from a blown-over trash can; and then, there on the northeast corner of Eighty-first Street, just as Penelope was turning toward Broadway, on a freshly paved square of sidewalk, she discovered #23.

MOE WAS HERE

Penelope bet she was the first kid in the neighborhood to find it! She'd definitely beaten Nathaniel. Served him right! She swooped down to get a closer look. What did Moe write his name with? A stick? His finger? She dipped her second finger inside the first line of the "M." Wow! It would take three of her thumbs to fill one line. If Moe used a finger, he was probably a giant. . . .

Just then, a heavy panting sound came from behind her. They were sloppy, slurry breathing sounds. And snapping to attention, Penelope became aware of what she must look like sitting in the middle of a city sidewalk. A skimpy girl. Vulnerable. All alone. You always heard stories about New York City kids getting mugged . . . or followed . . . or kidnapped. This kid in her class, Billy Stern, had been mugged five times! Penelope said a silent good-bye to the ten dollars in her pocket and whipped her head around. . . .

She was face-to-face with a frothy pink tongue, which, when you think about it, really meant that she was face-to-tongue.

The tongue hung from the open mouth of a shaggy brown dog attached to a long red leash. Penelope's eyes traced the leash up gray sweatpants splattered with paint, up the sleeve of a patchy olive green army jacket covered in different colored buttons, up the long, pale neck of a girl. At least Penelope thought it was a girl. It was hard to tell because of the blue corduroy baseball hat that covered her forehead and hit the rims of gigantic heart-shaped sunglasses.

The sunglasses had been very popular over the summer. They would have been the most normal part of the outfit had they not been missing one lens, so that one eye hid behind black plastic and the other, a brown coffee bean of an eye, stared flatly ahead.

"S-sorry," Penelope stumbled, untwisting herself and standing all the way up. The dog's tongue lapped at her leg and she stepped back, bumping smack into a short, bald man wielding a metal shopping cart full of brown grocery bags. A green apple flew out of a bag as the wagon hit the curb and the dog lunged for it, expertly snaring it in her teeth.

"Sorry!" called Penelope as the bald man teetered away, cursing under his breath. Penelope watched as he rolled his cart unevenly across the street. The light turned from yellow to red before he could get across, and a van beeped impatiently.

The strange girl chomped on a wad of bubble gum, staring with her one visible eye at Penelope. "Why?" she asked.

Huh? thought Penelope. "Why what?"

"Why are you sorry?" The girl blew a bubble. It popped, and she peeled it off her nose.

"I was in your way. I made that guy lose an apple," Penelope dully explained, not entirely sure why she was still standing there.

The gum sloshed in the girl's mouth when she talked. "It's a free country. You can stand where you want. And apples are cheap. Plus, look how much Sylvia Hempel likes it." Hearing her name, the dog lifted her snout in the air, crunching gleefully.

What kind of name for a dog is Sylvia Hempel? thought Penelope.

"You shouldn't feel you have to say sorry all the time. My philosophy is only say what you mean. So, I say sorry if I'm really sorry. And that's not very often."

"Well, I like to be polite," Penelope replied, if not a little smugly. She was pleased to have a response.

But the strange girl wasn't fazed. She just grinned and pointed to a cluster of buttons on her jacket. There was one with a peace sign on it, another that said: **WHEN THE GOING GETS TOUGH, I GET TOUGHER.**

But the button the girl was pointing her stubby finger at read: **POLITICS ARE NOT POLITE.** Penelope had no idea what that meant.

Some people can make you feel a certain way just by looking at you. With her one uncovered eye, this girl made Penelope feel like there was a big joke that everyone except Penelope was in on. It wasn't a feeling she particularly liked. "So, you're into Moe? I think he's a genius. People don't get that he's making a statement. I think that's the most important thing: making a statement. I try to make one every day." She pointed to another button on her jacket. In thick blue letters, it said: **IT'S NOT UNKIND TO SPEAK YOUR MIND.** "I think that's important, don't you?" Penelope didn't say anything, which didn't stop the girl from continuing. "So I heard a rumor Moe's really Kip Harwood."

When Penelope didn't respond, the girl said: "Oh, do you not know who that is? He's this really important artist who lives downtown. I think it might be him. What do you think?" Penelope shrugged. "Not much of a detective, are you? You're no Miss Marple. Oh, you don't know who that is, either? Wow! You mean you don't read Agatha Christie? I've read every single one. Twice. I like Hercule Poirot better than Miss Marple. He's the other detective."

Penelope had no idea what this girl was talking about. And she had no idea why she was still standing on the sidewalk listening to her. So when Sylvia Hempel tossed the apple core at the girl's dirty sneakers and the girl went to pick it up, Penelope stole away, tearing across the street just as the light was turning red.

"Hey! What's your name?" called the girl.

Penelope kept running.

A crazy person! Penelope had just spent five minutes talking to a crazy person! She was a city kid, warned all her life not to talk to strangers, let alone crazy ones!

"Sylvia Hempel says thanks for the apple!" the girl cackled. "See? She's very polite!"

As Penelope jogged toward Broadway, she thought she could hear Sylvia Hempel's toenails clicking behind her, but maybe she was just being paranoid.

Baronet had video games upstairs, and Stacy and Penelope shopped for school supplies to the sound of asteroids smashing. They needed graph paper and protractors for Algebra, composition books for English, and three-by-five index cards for Fundamental Languages, a class in which they studied seven languages in one year (that way, come eighth grade, they'd be prepared to pick a language to study through high school).

Penelope stood before the pen display. She tried a pink felt-tip marker, drawing a little squiggle on the pad of paper they kept for sampling. Someone had written in thick blue scrawl **School Sux**. It reminded Penelope of Moe #23. "I heard Moe might really be this famous downtown artist," she told Stacy.

"Really? Who told you that?"

"Hmmmm, uh, well, I don't remember," fumbled Penelope, feeling funny — for some reason — about mentioning her encounter with the strange girl.

Stacy skimmed her hand along a row of plastic binders. "Well, I heard 'Moe Was Here' really means 'Worship the Devil.'"

Penelope drew a heart with a green ballpoint. "What does that mean?"

"That it's not like one weirdo writing his name, it's a bunch of people, like a cult. They write 'Moe Was Here' 'cause it's code for 'Worship the Devil.'"

"Who would do that?" Penelope put an arrow through the heart.

"I don't know. Creepy people."

"Creepy how?" Penelope switched to a peach highlighter.

"Just creepy," Stacy said, annoyed.

"But how?"

"What does it make a difference? Creepy is creepy."

"How do you know it's not one guy?"

"Why do you have to be so dense? Even if it *is* one guy, he's still a creep. Anyone who writes his name all over the city has serious problems. You know that movie about the insane asylum where they give that crazy guy a lobotomy? That's what they should do to Moe." Stacy paused to look at the price tag on a plastic zippered pencil case. "I mean, IF he exists."

Penelope wondered if a day would go by when she didn't ask somebody to define something. "What's a lobotomy?" she asked, returning the highlighter to its place and moving toward the composition books.

"An operation where they make you brain dead. Like a zombie." Stacy picked up a packet of index cards. "You'd better work on your vocabulary. We're gonna have SATs."

"I thought not till eleventh grade," said Penelope.

"Yeah, but you should start now," Stacy declared in her most authoritative way.

It was nearly evening, and Penelope walked home with a brisk, determined step, clutching the bag from Baronet against her chest.

New school supplies. New teachers. New kids. New Moes. New mother's helper. New, new, new. When she wasn't having strange encounters with crazy girls and their dogs, there was no street more comforting than West End Avenue, and Penelope basked in the familiarity of the ten blocks between Baronet and home. The awnings from apartment buildings cast cool shadows on the sidewalk, and she made a game of speeding underneath them as quickly as possible so she could get back into the sun.

She didn't know what she expected to find at home, but a totally calm dinner scene was not it. *Shouldn't Jenny be just a little bit worried?* Instead, she just smiled serenely and said, "Hi, you get what you needed? Ready for dinner? We're having breaded chicken. Nathaniel said it was your favorite."

Nathaniel's face burst into a maniacal grin. Breaded chicken was *his* favorite.

"Seventh grade. Big year. Lots of homework, I bet." Jenny was talking to Penelope, but her brother answered.

"I have lots of homework!" he crooned. Nathaniel always acted like this when he was around new people; like a total show-off.

"Eight-year-olds do *not* have real homework." Penelope stabbed at a niblet of corn.

"I do! I have to do my workbook!" Nathaniel took a jubilant chomp of a dinner roll. Crumbs spattered his front.

"One dumb workbook page is *not* homework. It'll take you two minutes, and then you'll get a gold star."

"Shut up."

"You shut up."

"What are you gonna do if I don't."

"Give you a lobotomy, that's what!"

"What's a logodomy?"

"A lobotomy! Look it up, stupid!"

"I'm not stupid. And I have homework. I do."

The air between them filled with Penelope's urge to slug him.

"I don't know. Seems to me homework is homework," offered Jenny. She was kneeling on the floor wiping up Nathaniel's crumbs.

Who asked you? thought Penelope. *Go away. Go away. Go away.*

"Yeah!" Nathaniel clapped. "Homework is homework is homework is homework."

Penelope shoveled her dinner into her mouth in record time, then announced that she had to go do her homework, her *real* homework, looking directly at Nathaniel when she said it. She was halfway down the hallway when Nathaniel started singing. It was one of his more annoying habits, inventing songs and singing them in the loudest, most babyish voice.

"Homework is homework is homework.
I've got homework!
Penelope's got more than me!
Yeah, right! We'll see!
She should get a logodomy!"

Jenny laughed a tinkly little laugh. Jenny and Nathaniel could become best friends, for all Penelope cared; she didn't want any part of it.

She lay on her bed and thought about Moe: *What if Moe was a zombie? And what if there were a million Moes?*

There they were! Marching down Riverside Drive! Armed with pens! Writing their names on the sidewalk!

She imagined doormen running for cover, mothers kicking off their high-heeled pumps, hurling brief-cases and purses into the air, fathers hanging off No PARKING signs, tan trench coats fluttering in the wind. . . .

She fell asleep with a head full of zombies, and woke up several hours later to discover it was midnight and she was still wearing her clothes. She had a good six hours of homework to do, which meant if she started now, she'd be finished by the time she had to get ready for school. She even had an Algebra quiz to study for. Dr. Alvin's warnings — *don't get behind, catching up is very difficult* — were the last words she heard before she fell back to sleep.

A Quiz for Penelope B. Schwartzbaum

Prepared by Penelope B. Schwartzbaum

Have you ever had a boyfriend? No.

Do you want a boyfriend? ???????????????? (That's my answer.)

Do you want a new mother's helper? No!!!!!!!

Do you think it's really unfair that you have a new mother's helper? Yes!!!!!!

How many mother's helpers have you had: 17

Favorite mother's helper: Ivy

Second-favorite mother's helper: Stevie

Worst mother's helper: Beverly (French people are weird!)

What do you think of your little brother? He's a brat. (Nathaniel, if you're reading this, that means you.)

From Penelope B. Schwartzbaum's Book of Lists
Moe Was Heres — Page Three

14. phone booth on 77th and West End

15. outside Harry's Shoes

16. in front of Burger King

17. under awning of Big Apple Supermarket

18. on back table at Pizza Joint (scratched in)

19. in front of Broadway Nut Shop

20. on the side of Morris Brothers

21. inside lobby of Loews 83rd Street movie theater

22. on stairs to subway at 72nd Street and Broadway

23. 81st and West End — in sidewalk

Chapter Six

Shirley Commack was not in a good mood. "Stacy Commack!" she yelled. "Sometimes I think I don't even know you."

"Watch, she's gonna have a fit," Stacy whispered to Penelope. It wasn't strange for Shirley Commack to have a fit; she did so at least twice a day. But she usually tried to keep them out of public places. Either she couldn't help herself or she'd decided that Empire Szechuan no longer counted as a public place since she and Stacy ate half their meals there.

"What do you mean Oberlin College is an 'abnormal' institution for me to have attended? And what's this college obsession? You're twelve. Last year you were playing jacks, now you're — what? — pledging a sorority and picking a major?"

"I haven't played jacks since I was eight."

"That's not the point."

"I'm just saying —"

"You're just *saying* that the college I went to — where my political views were shaped, where I made all of my friends, where I met your father, for god's sake — you're just saying the institution I consider closest to my heart is abnormal. And what does this mean, 'abnormal'?"

"It means I just wouldn't want to go to school in Ohio. And it's not Ivy League."

"Ivy League is normal?"

"Normal for kids at Elston."

"Kids at Elston don't go *anywhere else* for college?"

"The ones who don't get such good grades go to other schools."

"I see. So, let me get this straight. 'Normal' means you are a wealthy kid, you grow up in New York City, and you go to Harvard because you get good grades in middle school and high school and plan ahead."

Stacy shrugged.

"You realize that's *not* normal. *Normal* people go to whatever college they can afford, if they go to college at all. *Normal* people don't have half the privileges you and your friends have. *Normal* people —"

Stacy cut her off. "I *said* 'normal for Elston,' Mom. I know I'm privileged. You've been telling me that my whole life. It's not my fault."

"It's not your fault, but it's not your —" Shirley Commack stopped herself. "Oh, forget it. I know you don't want to hear it. I just hope someday you realize there are no such things as normal and abnormal. And since when is a twelve-year-old a barometer for anything having *anything* to do with normal?"

"Stop calling me that," said Stacy.

"Stop calling you what?"

"A twelve-year-old."

"You *are* a twelve-year-old."

"You say it like it's a bad thing."

"A bad thing? It's a great thing! Don't you think I'd love to be twelve again? To have no responsibilities? To —"

"But, Mom, I *have* responsibilities!"

"Yes, to grow up at a reasonable pace. Not at this super-accelerated-head-straight-for-the-investment-banking-job-and-the-apartment-on-Park-Avenue pace. You're right. It's not your fault. It's that school you go to. I'm pulling you out."

Stacy rolled her eyes at Penelope as if to say she'd heard this all before. Shirley Commack was always threatening to pull her out of Elston Prep and dump her at the local public school. Not that she could; the custody agreement between Clay and Shirley Commack stipulated that Stacy could live full-time with Shirley as long as she attended Clay Commack's alma mater, Elston Prep.

"At least you'll have some diversity! Make a friend whose parents don't have stock portfolios and houses in the Hamptons. No offense, Penelope."

"My parents don't have a house in the Hamptons." She wasn't sure about the stock portfolio.

"I know, honey." She reached across the table to pat Penelope's hand.

"Fine," said Stacy. "Take me out of Elston Prep. I'll go live with Dad in L.A."

Shirley Commack poked at a dumpling with her chopstick. "You'd like that, wouldn't you? All those clothes! All that superficial crap! Get this? The paper's running a story about a new surgical procedure where they suck the fat out of your body with a huge straw. Whatever happened to eating healthy? Exercising?"

Penelope dunked her spoon in the hot-and-sour soup.

"No," Shirley Commack said, "people would rather stick a vacuum into their thighs and suck out all the extra glop."

Penelope put the spoon back in the bowl without taking a sip.

Penelope knew that Shirley Commack drove Stacy crazy, but she liked her. Sure, she agreed with Stacy that her mom's hair was too frizzy. And, yeah, she thought some of her habits were weird: like not getting out of her robe until dinnertime; like eating candy corn for breakfast; and not believing in credit cards, but never having cash on her.

But there were great things, too. One, she had a secret language with her cat, Mitzi. Two, she paid for Bernice to go to college at night. And three, she loved Chinese food. "God *knows* what's in that stuff," was what Mrs. Schwartzbaum always said when Penelope asked to order it in.

"So, if Oberlin's *too abnormal* for you, where, pray tell, are you considering going?"

"I'm looking into a lot of places," answered Stacy. "Yale, University of Pennsylvania, Cornell."

Shirley Commack nodded at her daughter with a bemused expression, then turned to Penelope. "Are you equally infected with the collegiate fever?"

Penelope had a mouth full of food, and Stacy took the opportunity to answer for her. "She'll try to go wherever I go," she said.

"Oh, will she?" asked Shirley Commack.

"We're best friends," replied Stacy, as if that answered everything. Penelope concentrated on the sweet-and-sour chicken, which was a particularly fluorescent shade of pink.

The waiter arrived to ask if they wanted anything else. "No," said Shirley Commack, "just the check," which he brought back promptly along with a tray of fortune cookies and sliced oranges. "I think this college thing could be an editorial," she mused, reaching into her pocket for money. "How they put the pressure on kids so young, and how it affects education. . . . The hook could be: Does anyone learn for learning's sake?"

"Whatever, Mom, just as long as you don't mention me," muttered Stacy, watching her mom shuffle through a wad of wrinkled bills.

"One, two, oh good, here's a five, so that's seven." Shirley Commack unfolded more bills. "Whoopee, another five! It's seventeen total, so what should I leave for the tip?"

Stacy had already calculated it.

"Oh, well, I'm a little short, then. I'm sure they'll understand. I'll bring Ling Tan the rest when we come back tomorrow." Stacy's face turned a deep crimson. "Oh, don't be so easily embarrassed. It happens to everyone." Except it didn't happen to Stacy, who actually kept her money in a wallet. She handed her mother the extra cash. "Well, at least you know I'm good for it," Shirley Commack said, laughing.

On the way back from Empire Szechuan, Shirley Commack stopped to call her editor from a pay phone, while Penelope and Stacy gazed at the jewelry on display in the window of P.S. I Love You. "Do you think I'll look like I'm copying if I get the ones Annabella wore today?" Stacy asked, pointing to a pair of fuchsia feather earrings. "It's not fair, because I thought about getting them a really long time ago."

It was happening more and more that Penelope had no idea how to respond to questions Stacy posed. Usually she just said what she thought Stacy wanted to hear. "I'm sure no one will notice," she assured her.

"Really?"

"Uh-huh."

Penelope waited outside while Stacy bought the earrings. "Where'd my college-bound daughter go?" Shirley Commack asked when she was off the phone.

Penelope pointed inside the store.

"I rue the day her father gave her that credit card," groaned Shirley Commack, gazing through the store window at her daughter. "Look at her buying accessories like a grown woman. When did twelve-year-olds get so old?"

A Quiz for Penelope B. Schwartzbaum

by Penelope B. Schwartzbaum

Extra-Credit Question

(Answer and Destroy Immediately!!!!)

What do you do when you realize you and your

best friend don't match?

A. Nothing.

B. Nothing.

C. Nothing.

D. All of the Above.

Answer: D — All of the Above!

Chapter Seven

Annabella and Pia cast menacing shadows over the lunch table.

"Nice earrings, Stacy."

The bite of turkey sandwich in Penelope's mouth turned to paper as Pia lowered her face to meet Stacy's and repeated herself.

"She said, 'Nice earrings, Stacy.'"

Stacy, who'd been eating a corn muffin, looked like she was going to choke. "Thanks," she said, and coughed.

Annabella peered down at her immaculate white cotton sweater, grimaced, and flicked an imaginary crumb from her chest. "Say it, don't spray it," she hissed. Stacy's face turned red, as if she were being strangled by invisible hands.

"So, where'd you get those nice earrings, Stacy? P.S. I Love You? They're sooooo nice." Pia said "so" as if it were a twelve-syllable word.

Stacy didn't say anything. "I don't think she got the point," remarked Pia.

Annabella had a soft lilt to her voice, so that even when she was saying something mean or embarrassing (and oftentimes she was), you didn't figure it out until you were thinking about it later. "I agree, Pia," she said. "I don't think she got the point."

It was funny how *big* people could seem in some situations, and how *small* they could seem in others. Under Annabella's gaze, Stacy positively shrank. "What? What's the point?" croaked Stacy, still struggling to swallow.

Pia's large face zoomed in to meet Stacy's. "You could have called Annabella to ask if she minded. It's rude — don't you think? — to buy the same earrings."

"I-I bought these before. I just waited awhile to wear them," lied Stacy, fidgeting in her chair to distance herself from Pia.

"Yeah, well, the more people who own something, the less its market value," spat Pia. Her dad owned a mall in New Jersey, so she knew a lot about the fashion industry.

Annabella Blumberg's left hand had a knack for finding its way to her left hip, which was perpetually jutting out; it gave the impression that — even if you were telling the truth — she didn't believe a word you said. "And what if I'd been wearing them today? That would have been pretty embarrassing. Did you think about that?"

"Well, sorry," squirmed Stacy, who, unlike Penelope, *didn't* have a tendency to apologize when it wasn't necessary, and clearly thought she was in the wrong. "I'll take them off," she offered, reaching for the earrings.

Annabella tilted her head to the left so her shiny brown hair flipped over her left eye. She looked straight out of a blow-dryer ad. "No need," she told Stacy. "It's too late now. But I accept your apology." There was an awkward silence until Stacy said thank you. "No problem," said Annabella with regal flourish. "And, by the way, they look nice on you."

"Oh, no, but they look better on you," Stacy said.

Satisfied that Annabella had gotten what she wanted, Pia declared that they needed to go, referencing a mysterious meeting regarding The Pledge. "Oh, and Penelope?" she added, her back turned. "No one wants your stinking fries. Don't be such a pig." Penelope hadn't realized it, but since Pia's arrival, she'd been cupping her hands protectively over her lunch tray. She moved her hands to the side lamely, then picked up a fry. It was cold and soggy.

In a matter of minutes, Stacy had experienced terror, relief, and gratitude, and it took several moments for her to collect herself: She took four long sips of soda. She wiped a napkin across her forehead. She readjusted the barrettes holding back her curly hair. She swept stray corn muffin crumbs from her lap. She dabbed her lips with Blistex. Then, she exploded in fury. "That was all your fault," she roared.

Penelope turned her head, half-expecting to see that Pia had returned to the table, that Stacy was screaming at someone other than herself. But no one else was there. "What d-did I-I do?" she stammered.

"You know what you did," steamed Stacy.

"I didn't tell them you were wearing the earrings!"

"That's not it."

"Then what?"

"You tell me."

Stacy could be tricky when she was angry.

"I don't know why you're mad," Penelope balked.

"Think about it!"

"I can't think of anything."

"Think harder!"

"I don't know. 'Cause I told you to get the earrings?"

"See, you admit it!"

"I didn't *tell* you to. I gave you my opinion!"

"Yeah, well, it was the wrong one."

"Opinions can't be wrong."

"Uh-huh," said Stacy blandly. She reached for her right ear and unhooked the earring. She reached for the left.

Penelope gaped. "You're taking them off?"

"They're so heavy, they're killing my ears." Stacy rubbed at the inflamed holes in her puffy earlobes. "I think I have an infection. You want to wear them?"

"My ears are closed up. You know that," muttered Penelope. The thought — *that bad thought!* — was zipping through Penelope's head: *We don't match. We don't match. We don't match.* She watched Stacy pocket the earrings and only half-heard her when she said, "Oh, and we have to sign The Pledge."

♥♥♥♥♥

Mr. Bobkin and his belly galumphed from desk to desk, returning the quiz. As Mr. Bobkin's stomp got closer, Penelope made sure not to make eye contact with the teacher. When he laid the quiz on her desk, she shut her eyes before she could see the grade, and slapped her hand over the right corner of the page. She thought, *If I don't see it, it doesn't exist.*

But of course that wasn't true.

Penelope unglued her fingers so she could see a speck of what was underneath.

Please be the triangle tip of an A!

Nope. No tip. A slight curve.

Could it be the bulging top of a B?

If I pray this is a B, it will be a B, she thought. *Please be a B! Please be a B!*

But it looked more like a C.

Maybe Mr. Bobkin's pen slipped. Or maybe he'd written in lowercase. Maybe it was a lowercase A.

Penelope moved her hand. She clenched her eyelids shut, then opened them. The light made tiny little pink and purple spots on the page, and it took her a second to focus. It was a . . .

C.

Not only a C.

C–.

Mr. Bobkin used the remaining class time to go over the quiz. Why had X times that equaled that, and next time everybody should make sure to remember the tricks with the zeroes, and don't forget about negative numbers and . . . if they didn't understand fractions, they better come to see him and . . . Penelope felt the daze overcome her, and she just couldn't listen any longer.

She studied the graffiti on the desk. There were some new additions: **M.W. = 2COOL4SKOOL. P.H. RULES JV FIELD HOCKEY.** Then, written in blue ballpoint ink on the bottom right-hand corner was a list:

BIGGEST SNOBS AT ELSTON PREP
#1   Pam Ascher
#2   Kimmie Sheck
#3   Mickey Ling

Penelope looked each way, like a stray cat before making a mad dash under a car. Bobkin and his large belly were facing the blackboard. No one was looking at her. In a blur of movement, yet with a steady hand, as if this were something she'd done a million times before, Penelope wrote: #4 Annabella Blumberg. And then: #5 Pia Smith.

If five seconds later someone had asked Penelope who'd written those names on the desk, she would have said she had no idea. And she wouldn't have been lying. Because as soon as she did it, she promptly forgot.

When the bell rang and Mr. Bobkin growled,

"Dismissed," Penelope crumpled up the quiz and crammed it into her backpack, unintentionally puncturing it with the pointy end of her protractor. She'd ignore its existence until, weeks later, shredded, the quiz crept its way in between the pages of her Earth Science textbook.

"Don't worry," said Ben. "I messed up, too." He held up his quiz for Penelope to see. Inside the circle at the top of the page it said: B–. "Maybe we could study together sometime. Where do you live?"

"Ninetieth and West End," Penelope told him.

"Cool! My old school is on the West Side. Do you ever play video games at Baronet? I miss that. Shoot, I miss the whole West Side. My old school, too. You know, it's not so easy being a new kid here."

A curl inched down his forehead. It reminded Penelope of a caterpillar.

"That sucks," replied Penelope, though when she thought about it later — and she did, *a lot* — she knew there were a lot better things she could have said. Like: "It's not so easy being an old kid here, either."

But she was never going to say that. Or anything to Ben. At least not anytime in the near future. Because after gym, Stacy and Penelope signed The Pledge. Penelope signed her name in scratchy, minuscule letters that were difficult to decipher — as if somehow a secret part of her knew she didn't really want to do it.

After all, if it wasn't really her signature, it wasn't really her, right?

Chapter Eight

If Mrs. Schwartzbaum was tired on a regular day, she was even *more* tired when Mr. Schwartzbaum was away traveling on business. In fact, she got so tired, she replaced "I'm so tired" with "I'm wiped out." Or "I'm a wreck." Or "I'm beyond exhausted. How can one person work an eighty-hour week *and* run a household?"

But something strange happened the week Penelope's father went to Belgium. Mrs. Schwartzbaum stopped saying she was tired. She even stopped *looking* tired. It was kind of like . . . she woke up.

It was positively odd. Mrs. Schwartzbaum never came home before dinner. But, three days into Mr. Schwartzbaum's trip, she got home at 5 P.M. — just as Penelope and Nathaniel were fighting over what to watch on the kitchen television, *One Day at a Time* or *The Flintstones.*

Mrs. Schwartzbaum arrived home with flushed cheeks, a smile on her face, and a silk scarf tied around her head to protect her new hairstyle from the wind. Carlos trailed behind her, a bouquet of brown and purple shopping bags in each hand. "Remember, Carlos, you promised! No telling Herbert I bought the entirety of Bloomie's *and* Bergdorf Goodman?" giggled Mrs.

Schwartzbaum, slipping a ten-dollar bill into Carlos's hand.

It turned out she had popped in only for an hour. She had a dinner meeting at a fancy French restaurant called Lutèce and she needed to freshen up. "I'm going to have to be careful with all this wining and dining." She sighed, removing a new red Calvin Klein pencil skirt from its lavender tissue-paper wrapping. "I don't want to turn into a tons-o'-fun."

Penelope perched herself on the edge of the bathtub and watched her mother do her hair and makeup. "I saw a new guy at La Coupe today. I think he worked wonders, don't you?"

"It's redder," answered Penelope as her mother fluffed her hair for the mirror.

"Yes, well, why not?" Mrs. Schwartzbaum laughed. "A little touch-up never hurt anybody. I needed some luster." She spritzed her head with a new hairspray she'd bought at the salon. It made the bathroom smell like the inside of a swimming pool.

She brushed a coral shadow onto her eyelids and told Penelope about the client she'd be having dinner with. He was an art buyer for one of New York City's largest auction houses; at a mere twenty-nine, he was considered a whiz kid. His name was Fred Sunderstein, but Mrs. Schwartzbaum said it so fast, it sounded like Fred Something. "He's an inspiration. The energy he has, I tell you, he's indefatigable."

"What does indefatigable mean?" asked Penelope.

"Not able to get tired," answered Penelope's mother. She applied a dab of peach gloss to her lips, then pursed them into a kiss. "I don't know what his secret is, but he's got the energy of ten men. Maybe it's that he's twenty-nine. Or that he doesn't have any obligations."

"What do you mean, obligations?"

"I mean," replied Mrs. Schwartzbaum, taking one last look in the mirror, "a wife. A family. Kids."

She made the kiss lips again and blotted them with a white tissue.

Then she was gone.

Penelope, Nathaniel, and Jenny ate hamburgers on English muffins for dinner. As was typical, Nathaniel babbled and sang throughout the meal, and Penelope slammed her food down her throat so fast, she could barely taste it. On Nathaniel's request, they had Purple Cows for dessert. Purple Cows were vanilla ice cream mixed with grape soda. They'd been a favorite of Ivy's.

It was becoming a tradition that Jenny played music while they had dessert. Penelope suspected it was because she couldn't bear hearing Nathaniel sing. They were records by people Penelope had never heard of, and usually they were from England. Jenny's favorite was a guy with a weird name, Elvis Costello, who looked an awful lot like Penelope's Earth Science teacher. Jenny said her roommate at college was friends with Elvis's manager's little sister, which meant she got tapes of albums before they even came out. "He's totally original, don't you think?" Jenny asked Penelope. Penelope didn't know what to say. She couldn't understand a word the guy sang, and even when she could decipher the words, she didn't know what they meant: "I'm giving you a longing look! Every day I write the book! Captured here in my quotation marks!" Nathaniel couldn't figure it out, either, but that didn't stop him from humming along and bopping up and down as Purple Cow dribbled from his chin. "Even in a perfect world where everyone was equal!" sang the record. "Every day I write the book!"

Mrs. Schwartzbaum got home just before eleven. There were the familiar sounds: the clicking of heels, the clump of her pocketbook dropping to the floor, the swish of a trench coat being tossed off. But they were followed by an unfamiliarly giddy "Jenny, let me tell you, it was fab-u-lous."

Penelope entered the kitchen to find her mother and Jenny sitting across from each other at the table. Jenny was sipping from a mug of tea, and Mrs. Schwartzbaum, from a tiny crystal glass, the kind they used for holidays or when Penelope's grandparents came from Florida to visit. Inside the glass was a dark rust-colored liquid that shimmered golden under the kitchen's overhead halogen lamp.

"Hi, darling," called Mrs. Schwartzbaum with a grin. Penelope asked what she was drinking, and Mrs. Schwartzbaum explained it was a scotch Penelope's father had brought from Scotland.

"Are you going to get drunk?" Penelope knew it was probably a dumb question to ask, but she didn't know very much about alcohol. The Schwartzbaums weren't big drinkers. In fact, any fancy bottles of alcohol brought back by Mr. Schwartzbaum were usually reserved as Christmas gifts for Carlos.

"Of course not, silly!" Mrs. Schwartzbaum laughed. "I just need a little nightcap. Something to get me to sleep."

But this was the woman who claimed she could fall asleep standing up! Maybe her mother was drunk! Maybe she just didn't realize it!

The only drunk person Penelope had ever seen was Mr. Pearl, from Apartment 15J, who'd once fallen asleep on the lobby sofa with a Happy New Year party hat over his nose and a purple streamer tied around his head. He'd looked like a giant blob of Silly Putty, and Penelope had found it unspeakably funny. In fact, for weeks after, she and Stacy had stumbled around, giggling uproariously and slurring, "I'm drunk. I'm drunk."

Well, Mrs. Schwartzbaum wasn't acting like that, so she probably wasn't drunk. But something *was* off. Penelope listened as her mother listed the menu at Lutèce. Her eyes practically glittered at the recollection of the filet mignon and duck confit, not to mention the lobster Provençal. And Fred Something was such good company! He knew just about everybody in the restaurant! An architect had sent over complimentary flutes of champagne; the famous art collector Bea Levin had come over to say hello; and several of Fred Something's classmates from Harvard were at the next table. They were all investment bankers, which meant they were terrifically wealthy but not half as interesting as Fred.

"I gotta say, there are a lot of benefits to going to Harvard," mused Mrs. Schwartzbaum. "Just look at the connections. All those guys will buy art from Fred. And they'll tell their friends and —" Mrs. Schwartzbaum interrupted herself, as if she'd just remembered who she was talking to. "You know, Penelope, you could have those opportunities, too. Elston Prep is your ticket into a school like Harvard. Keep your grades up and I can't imagine you'll have a problem. And I'm sure Fred would write you a recommendation.

"Oh, and bad news. I can't go shopping with you over the weekend. I know this is the third time I've canceled. I know you're disappointed, but I just have too much work. I do have a gift for you. It's —" Mrs. Schwartzbaum interrupted herself again to take a sip of her drink. She shot Penelope a mysterious look. "Hand me my pocketbook, will you?"

Inside Mrs. Schwartzbaum's pocketbook were two

charge cards — one for Bloomingdale's and one for Bergdorf Goodman — in the name of Penelope B. Schwartzbaum. "Now, I'm trusting you to show restraint," her mother warned. "You know, some parents might not approve of a girl your age getting her own credit cards. But I see it as a gift for both of us."

Penelope traced her fingertip along the raised letters spelling out her name.

"You get the gift of shopping for yourself. And I get the gift of time." She swallowed the remainder of her drink and let out a contented sigh. "Clothes and time. Two things a girl can't have enough of."

Before going to bed, Penelope showered, changed into the sweatpants and T-shirt she wore as pajamas, then returned to her homework. She still had Social Studies to do, but she sat at her desk staring at her new credit cards. On the backs were clean white bands where she was supposed to sign her name. She thought about The Pledge, and how — on these — she'd have to put her *real* signature. But what was her real signature? Would she use the puffy P? The script S? Or a print S that looped at the bottom to connect to the C?

A soft knock on the door disrupted her thoughts. "Come in," she called, and there was Jenny standing in the doorway with two steaming mugs of hot chocolate and a pocket full of elastic bands. "Hey, Pen, want me to crimp your hair for you?"

Penelope had planned on not liking Jenny — *she really had!* — but that night, as gentle fingers wove into her wet hair, she forgot that Jenny wasn't Ivy, that she was too old for a mother's helper, and finished her Social Studies homework.

"You have excellent handwriting," whispered Jenny, the last clump of Penelope's hair twisted between her fingers. The wet braids lay heavily on Penelope's head.

Stacy was wrong. Some people were too difficult *not* to like — no matter how hard you tried.

THE NO NEWKS NEWKSLETTER
(Get it? Newksletter! Ha-ha.)

BY: THE NEWKLEAR POWERS THAT BE

IF YOU ARE READING THIS, THAT MEANS YOU SIGNED THE PLEDGE! CONGRATS!!!!!!!!!!!

EDITORIAL
By L.L.

You need to pick what college you're going to go to (or going to *want* to go to) now. As in *right* now. If you have no idea, well, then, you are behind. I don't mean to scare you, but this is important.

7th-grade grades count on your transcript!!!!!!!!!! (Do you even know what a transcript is?)
Are you a Yalie? Do you root for the Tigers? (If you don't know that the Tigers are Princeton's football team . . . guess what? You're already behind!)

You gotta pick! Get ahead of the competition! (And you know who that is, right? Hint, hint . . . new kids!)

♥ ♥ ♥ ♥ ♥ ♥ ♥ ♥ ♥ ♥ ♥ ♥ ♥

GOSSIP ITEM
Who likes Annabella Blumberg? (As in *likes* likes . . .)

A. Richie Chernovsky
B. John Bart
C. Jerry C.
D. You Know Who You Are!!!

(Submit answers to P.S.)

♠ ♠ ♠ ♠ ♠ ♠ ♠ ♠ ♠ ♠ ♠ ♠ ♠

COMING NEXT ISSUE:
S.C.'s Style Report. What to wear if you're a No-Newker. The answer is not leg warmers over white tights! Sorry, you know who . . . (was that too mean?????)

Chapter Nine

September turned to October to November, and seventh graders traded their polo shirts for sweaters in cotton, cashmere, and angora; their walking shorts for khakis; their tube socks for argyles. Penelope and Stacy had gotten used to the new campus, and during their free periods they gravitated toward the benches outside the cafeteria foyer. There, No Newkers formed a line of down vests and Fair Isle sweaters and discussed the latest gossip, which these days was more than likely about Tillie Warner and how her parents were getting divorced.

Parents getting divorced wouldn't be a big deal, usually, but Bill and Cherry Warner were going through what promised to be — in Mrs. Schwartzbaum's words — *a horrific divorce,* the kind that made the New York papers because it involved a lot of money and *General Hospital*–style twists and turns.

With every day came another dreadful detail: Tillie's dad had an affair! He owned a chalet in Aspen that Tillie's mom didn't know about! He paid for his mistress's apartment in the Village! Cherry Warner was going to take him for everything he's worth — and more!

If the latest tidbit didn't come from the papers, it came from the Chapstick-smeared mouth of Vicki

Feld, who took to her role as Tillie's best friend with aplomb. Either she was harassing kids for gossiping about Tillie behind her back, or chastising them for getting the details wrong. *No, the woman wasn't his secretary! Yes, he's moving out. No, he's not taking Tillie with him!*

It was almost Thanksgiving break, the pressure of seventh grade was mounting, and Dr. Alvin was delivering her version of a pep talk. "Ladies and gentlemen, I know you're having a rough time. You're feeling overwhelmed. All I can say is: Get used to it."

Tillie sat directly in front of Penelope. The teacher paced the length of the room, Penelope stared at the back of Tillie's head. Tillie's habit of picking at her split ends had evolved into outright hair pulling. Strands fell out in clumps.

"If there's any consolation, it's that it's not going to get harder. We make seventh grade as difficult as possible so that we can identify which of you are not going to make it. There's no delicate way to put it: This year we're going to try to weed you out."

There was a television show Penelope used to watch when she was little, *The Magic Garden,* where the hosts Paula and Carole had to walk through a cartoon flower patch. All the flowers had smiley faces.

Penelope imagined her homeroom class as the flower patch: Tillie, Richie Chernovsky, Lillian Lang, their faces in the middle of floppy yellow-and-white petals on top of green stem bodies. And there her face was, in the middle of one of those hairy weeds — what do you call them? tumbleweeds? — getting ripped out of the soil. She could see bare hands pulling her up, knuckles red and knobby, fingernails digging into her droopy brown stalk. Whose hands were they? Dr. Alvin's?

"If the work's too hard, if you really can't cut it here, well, better you find out now. We'll be doing you a favor."

Penelope watched a clump of Tillie's wispy red hair waft to the floor.

"Oh, the poor thing," Mrs. Schwartzbaum remarked when, that evening, Penelope told her about Tillie's hair-tugging problems. "That makes me sad."

Here was something Penelope noticed: Like Vicki, no matter how much Mrs. Schwartzbaum talked about "feeling sad for Tillie and the Warners," she didn't look it. Not that her mother was *pleased* to hear about Tillie's parents' misfortunes; it was just that hearing about them didn't make a dent in her happy mood. It seemed that just about nothing could.

Penelope still wasn't used to seeing her mother so chipper. It was a phenomenon. Mr. Schwartzbaum had gone away on business, returned, then gone away again, and Mrs. Schwartzbaum was *still* as happy as ever. She seemed lively, perky even, she was full of stories — most of them about Fred Something:

"Fred Something has exquisite taste."
"Not only that, he's a trained chef!"
"He's got a Calder mobile. Do you know what that's worth?"
"He makes his own pasta and his own bread!"

There was so much Fred Something talk in the house, even Penelope had him on the brain. And she hadn't even met the guy! But she dreamed about him. Four nights in a row, in fact. She didn't know what the dream was about, only that Fred Something had been in it and he'd looked exactly like Rick from *General Hospital.*

It took Carlos arriving at the door with a package for Mrs. Schwartzbaum to make Penelope remember any of the dream's details.

It was a large box, wrapped in brown paper, and delivered directly from the Museum of Modern Art. Mrs. Schwartzbaum giddily tore open the package to discover that inside there was another box, this one covered in silver paper. And inside that box was one of the weirdest objects Penelope had ever seen: a bright orange circle with lots of little legs.

Apparently, it was a clock.

A clock! Penelope thought she might be remembering her dream. Something about Fred Something . . . and . . . Monica Quartermaine???

The clock was a gift from Fred Something, a very

expensive gift, according to Penelope's mother, with the artist's signature on the back. "It's too much," Mrs. Schwartzbaum gushed. "It's too much!"

Penelope remembered something in the dream about a digital watch. Or was it a pocket watch?

"Oh, I think we studied that clock in our modern design seminar," said Jenny when she emerged from the kitchen.

And they were wearing doctor's clothes!

"Yes, I believe I saw one of those at an exhibit," added Carlos, who'd stuck around to fix a loose wire in the intercom.

And they were in the operating room!

Nathaniel slid down the hall on his belly, making *vroom vroom* sounds as he wheeled a miniature Pontiac Firebird across the wood floor. "What kind of clock is that?" he asked.

And someone was wearing a mask. But who?

"This is a clock, but it's also art," explained his mother, skimming her finger along the clock's surface. "It's a very famous piece made by George Nelson, the designer. It's called the Sunburst Clock."

Oh, Monica was wearing a mask! But the weird thing was, when she took the mask off . . . she wasn't Monica. She was someone else. But who?

Nathaniel had many questions: "But how do you tell the seconds, and why is it orange?"

No! It couldn't be!

"How come Fred Something gave you a gift? It's not your birthday, Mommy."

Monica was . . .

"Is it Hanukkah already?"

Oh, my god.

"Am *I* going to get a gift? 'Cause I want Mattel Electronic Baseball."

Penelope thought she might puke.

Instead, she put her hands on her hips, stared at her little brother, and yelled, "Who cares what you want? And who cares about a dumb clock?!" The words "dumb clock" stuck in her throat like she'd swallowed a grape whole.

Nathaniel dropped his car to the floor, its wheels still turning as it took a sad jolt forward. "Sorry," he whispered.

"A Sunburst Clock is just 'a dumb clock,'" repeated Mrs. Schwartzbaum in a slow and punishing tone.

Penelope didn't have to look up to know that Carlos, Jenny, and her mother were looking at her. She could feel it! The six adult eyes burned into her, and she shuffled from foot to foot. She hadn't meant to call it a dumb clock, at least not out loud.

"I'm not sure how to account for that bizarre outburst, Penelope," said her mother. "I'll just assume you're tired." She turned away from her daughter and resumed talking in a chipper clip: "Oh, Carlos, Jenny, while you're both here. I wanted to let you know I'm having a tea Saturday. Carlos, if you're not on duty, can you tell whoever is? And, Jenny, I was wondering if you might want to serve. If not, I could ask the house-keeper. But if you want extra cash, I'd pay you hourly."

She turned back to Penelope. "Oh, and Penelope, I forgot to mention that a classmate of yours is coming. Her name is Cass. A new girl. Do you know her? She's accompanying her grandmother, Bea Levin. You know, the famous art collector? Perhaps I mentioned that she's a friend of Fred's. She has this giant modern sculpture garden."

Penelope tried to explain to her mother about The Pledge and how she wasn't supposed to talk to new kids, but Mrs. Schwartzbaum looked at her like she was talking gibberish and swung the conversation back to Bea Levin and her magnificent collection, which just might be as good as the Whitney's.

My Dream About Fred Something
By Penelope B. Schwartzbaum

Rick/Fred Something and Dr. Monica Quartermaine are wearing white doctors' coats. Also, green surgery uniforms like the ones on *M*A*S*H*. (I think they call them scrubs.) Rick/Fred Something reaches into the pocket of his white coat. He's got a velvet box. He gives it to Monica. Inside is this weird pocket watch like the rabbit in *Alice in Wonderland* has, only with diamonds. Rick/Fred Something says something dumb, like: "We'll always have time." Then Monica says: "We'll be together forever." "You mean you're leaving Alan?" asks Rick/Fred Something. "Yes," says Monica.

Rick/Fred Something leans in to kiss Monica. There's all this dumb music. He gets closer and closer and then it's so weird but Monica is wearing a surgical mask (like the doctors wear on *M*A*S*H*). Rick/Fred Something goes to untie it, and underneath the mask MONICA'S NOT MONICA. SHE'S MY MOM!!!!!!!

Chapter Ten

Penelope once heard her father say that a movement was successful when the backlash against it began. Well, then Annabella and Pia had something to be proud about, because a backlash against The Pledge — in the form of tiny little messages graffiti-ed in bathroom stalls around the school — was underway. Some messages were straight to the point:

THE PLEDGE SUX.

Some were a slightly more subtle:

NO NEWKS, NO WAY.

Seventh graders were discussing the messages almost as much as they were discussing Annabella's bat mitzvah and Tillie's parents' horrific divorce.

Penelope, Stacy, Vicki, and Tillie arrived on the second floor of Gritzfield Hall to find Annabella and Pia, flanked by Lillian and Annie, officiating outside the girls' bathroom. The way Annabella greeted them reminded Penelope of her uncle's wedding when the bride stood at the end of a receiving line and accepted kisses and congratulations from guests. Annabella wore a periwinkle sweater that gave her blue eyes a cloudy look, like jeans that had been accidentally bleached. "Hi, you guys," she chirped. "You're not gonna believe this one!" If Annabella was a leader besieged, well, she wasn't really acting like one — she seemed positively pleased by the turn of events.

Stacy and Vicki shoved their way past the swell of seventh graders, taking Penelope and Tillie with them. There, in the third stall, written on the wall in chunky black script, it said:

You say no newk,

I say puke.

"Whoa," said Stacy.

"Wow," said Vicki.

"Ha!" Tillie laughed under her breath, then covered it with a cough.

Annabella had gone to class, but Pia lingered outside the bathroom, chewing angrily on a pencil and staring deliberately at her clipboard. "Who do you think it is, Pia?" asked Stacy.

Pia's lips were covered in bits of yellow pencil,

and she wiped her mouth with the back of her hand. "I don't know, but I'm gonna find out," she answered.

"Some new kid, I'm sure," mumbled Vicki.

"I think it might be a bunch of new kids," suggested Stacy.

"Why?" asked Pia, sticking out her tongue to see if there was pencil on it.

"Lots of different handwriting," answered Stacy. "Also, think about it: *Nobody* we know would write on the walls."

They stood pondering this.

Pia put her tongue back in her mouth. "Yeah, well, whoever's doing it, they're gonna regret it. This is a really big deal."

"I've decided. Rick and Monica are gonna get married."

Stacy clicked off the television, punctuating her announcement with a burst of static. Tillie, Vicki, and Penelope had gone to Stacy's house after school, and they'd just watched the episode of *General Hospital* where Alan Quartermaine learned about Rick and Monica's affair.

Vicki didn't think this sounded right. "You mean you think she's going to divorce Alan?"

"Yeah, why not?"

"Monica would never divorce Alan."

"Why?"

"She'd have to move out of the mansion. That's why."

"I don't think Monica would stay married for money. She'll move out for love."

Vicki, playing the sensitive friend, shot Stacy an important stare as if to say they shouldn't talk about this stuff around Tillie. So they changed the subject. They started talking about boyfriends.

"I just feel so *abnormal* not having one," moaned Vicki.

"I know," said Stacy. "My stepsister has a boyfriend, and she's nine! I'm in seventh grade! It's not *normal*."

Penelope wondered: *Does Stacy want a boyfriend because she's normal or because it's normal to want a boyfriend. Is there a difference?*

Vicki and Stacy talked about curly hair versus straight hair on boys and whether it was better for boys to like sports or video games and did collecting baseball cards automatically make you a nerd? And what about liking *Star Trek*?

Penelope lay on the white shag rug in the middle of Stacy's floor and listened to this conversation as if she were lying on a towel in the middle of a crowded beach. She could hear fragments of sentences and select words — *pathetic, pitiful* — mingling with the hum of Bernice's vacuum cleaner. It wasn't until Stacy stood over her and shouted, "ARE YOU ALIVE?" that

Penelope realized an hour had gone by, Vicki and Tillie had gone home for dinner, and somehow she was lying facedown on the shag rug.

"You gotta go, space case. My dad's in town and he's taking me out to dinner. Sheesh, for a second I thought you were dead!"

"Hi, Pen," said Shirley Commack, who was walking in when Penelope was walking out. "You okay? You look out of it. Is my daughter on a college kick again? That stuff will fry your brains. If I were you, I'd just ignore it."

When Penelope exited the black iron gates of Stacy's building, she discovered Tillie Warner waiting for her. It was dark out, and under the streetlamp Tillie's hair glowed like an orange highlighter. Her green eyes were rimmed with red.

"Are you crying?" asked Penelope.

"No, allergies," wheezed Tillie. She pointed to the Christmas tree display on the corner; it was only November, but you could already buy a tree on several major cross streets. "Those give me asthma."

They stood silently for a moment. Penelope looked from the trees to Tillie to the sidewalk. Was that a Moe Was Here next to the fire hydrant? She took a step closer to check it out.

"What are you doing?" asked Tillie.

"Looking to see if Moe was here."

"Moe's crazy," sniffled Tillie, who, despite being from the Upper East Side, knew about the Upper West Side's most notorious graffiti artist. Then she added inexplicably, "But I don't mean crazy in a bad way."

What Penelope had thought was a Moe turned out to just be a scratch. "I didn't wait around to look for Moes," Tillie told her. "I want to talk to you."

"Me?"

"Yes, you."

The Christmas trees formed a tunnel on Seventy-ninth Street, and inside, the air was thick with pine. Four white sneakers sloshed along the wet sidewalk flecked with green needles, like white boats crossing a dark river covered in algae.

When she could breathe again, Tillie got right to the point. "Being best friends with someone is like being married," she said. "Have you ever thought that?"

Penelope told her she hadn't.

"One person's the boss, and the other is the follower. It's just like my parents. My dad was — I mean *is*, he *is* — this big bully, and my mom did everything he said." She corrected herself. "I mean does, *does everything he says.*"

They stopped at a red light.

"I used to ask her why she didn't stick up for herself. Guess what she said? That she couldn't be bothered! That it was too much work! Isn't that pathetic?"

Penelope wondered if she should nod and agree that Tillie's mom was pathetic. That might seem rude.

"It took, well, it took" — Tillie rolled up the sleeve of her coat to scratch a strawberry-sized collection of tiny red bumps on her wrist — "let's just say it took a lot for her to finally stick up for herself. He cheated on her, you know? Had an affair!"

"Like Rick and Monica on *General Hospital*," said Penelope.

Tillie scratched until the bumps were bloody. "Yeah, but Monica's a lot prettier than Rochelle. That's his" — she sucked on her finger, then spat out the word as if it were poison — "girlfriend. My mom waited so long to tell off my dad, he and Rochelle were practically doing it in her face. You know, he was buying Rochelle all these gifts and putting them on the credit card. He never bought my mom gifts!"

An image of the Sunburst Clock erupted in Penelope's head. She rubbed her eyes with her mittened hands as if that would get rid of it.

"Can you keep a secret?" Tillie asked Penelope. "You promise you won't tell anybody? Not even Stacy? I'm gonna ask Pia to cross my name off The Pledge. If Vicki doesn't want to be my best friend and Annabella disinvites me from her dumb bat mitzvah, I don't care. I'm having one next year and I just won't invite her. I won't invite any of them."

They reached the corner of Eighty-sixth Street,

and it was as if the walk had strengthened Tillie. With every block, she got more and more determined. She crossed her arms across her chest and stared purposefully at Penelope. "The way I see it, there are leaders and there are followers and then there's us. We're not even followers. We're followers of followers. And you know what that makes us?"

Penelope shook her head.

"Nobody," answered Tillie. "It makes us nobody."

The crosstown bus skidded to the curb. "If it doesn't bug you, then sorry I said anything. If it does bug you, well . . ." The doors to the bus opened.

"Hey, Tillie!" Penelope called out, because the idea had just struck her. "You don't know who wrote the stuff on the walls, do you?"

Tillie climbed a step. She turned and peered down at Penelope. She was having fun now, and her top lip curled into a snaky smile. "Maybe I do, maybe I don't," she teased.

A gust of wind blew between them.

"All I can say," added Tillie mysteriously, "is, the person writing on the walls is brave. Crazy, maybe. But brave."

The doors closed, and the bus began to move.

Penelope wove her way home, past men and women hulking with grocery bags and shopping carts. She swerved past a sobbing child beating the sidewalk with his fists, a pack of yapping white dogs mashed together in a tangle of leashes.

She thought: *These are my feet that are walking. These are my hands jammed in my pockets. These are my fingertips touching coins and lint. This is my thumb pressing into a wad of gum. I chewed that gum. I spit it out. I put it in a wrapper. I put it in my pocket. I'm what's walking down the street. I'm what's taking me home. AM I NOBODY?*

The next day, a new message appeared in the gym locker room. It said:

N = Nobody (except)
O = Obviously Idiotic
N = No Brains (who)
E = Everyone Hates (and are)
W = Wastes of Space (would be the)
K = Kind of Kids (who'd)
S = Sign The Pledge

"I don't get it," said Vicki.

"It's hard to read at first," said Stacy.

"Is it a poem?" asked Annabella.

"No," said Tillie. "It's a puzzle, an anagram. Read what's on the right side of the equals sign first. Then, look at the left. If you read that column going down, it says, 'NO NEWKS.'"

"Oh, yeah," they said as a chorus.

"How'd you figure that out so fast, Tillie?" asked Pia.

Tillie whipped her head around. "What's that supposed to mean, Pia?"

Pia tapped her pencil against her clipboard. "What? I can't ask a question, *Tillie*?"

"I didn't say that!"

"Well, you act like it's a crime!"

The five-minute warning bell clanged, and Annabella took it as an opportunity to have the last word. "The point is," she calmly intoned, "whoever is doing it will get in huge trouble. Not just with us, but with the school. Graffiti is a really big deal."

They headed to class.

Part Two

My Dream About Stacy and the Rope Ladder
By Penelope B. Schwartzbaum

Stacy and I used to go to her country house for two weeks every summer (when her dad and mom were together). There was a rope ladder in the playground nearby, the kind that hangs between two trees. Stacy climbed it every day, and I hated it. (It was boring and it hurt my hands!) Anyway, in the dream, we're on the first rung of the rope ladder. We're about to swing to the second one, and a crazy wind hits. The rope starts shaking.

"Keep going!" screams Stacy. But I can't. I fall and fall and fall and then I land in this squishy mound of brown dirt. Except it's not a mound, it's a pit. I'm in a hole below the earth. (I think we learned a fancy word for that in Earth Science, but I can't remember it.) I keep calling, "Stacy!"

I can barely see her. She's a little speck moving along a rope ladder.

I try to pull myself out, but the walls keep crumbling in my hands. And then I realize I'm not alone. There are lions in the pit! They're baby lions, they're so cute! But wait! Cubs still bite! I'm going to die! I scream to Stacy, but she's gone. She made it to the end. No one sees me! There's hot lion breath on my neck. I can feel whiskers on my shoulder. Then I wake up.

Chapter Eleven

Herbert and Denise Schwartzbaum had a tendency to argue for the first couple of days after one of Herbert's business trips, and on Saturday morning, after a restless night of sleep, Penelope woke up to sounds of her parents bickering.

"Denise, please, why are you starting?"

"I'm not starting. You're the one who's starting."

The digital clock blinked at her: 8:31 A.M. She mashed her face into the pillow. Maybe she could sleep for just a little bit more.

Mr. Schwartzbaum had returned from Portugal the night before with gifts: a collector's doll for her, a train set for Nathaniel, and chocolates, olive oil, and a tablecloth for her mother. The first thing he'd done upon entering the apartment — Carlos trailing behind him with his bags — was point at the Sunburst Clock. "What the hell is that?" he fumed. When Mrs. Schwartzbaum explained, he shook his head and sighed. "If that's art, then . . ." Herbert Schwartzbaum was such a busy man, he often didn't complete his sentences.

"Can we just not do this right now?"

"We can just not do anything right now."

Penelope mashed her face harder into the pillow until her nose hurt. *I'll just stay this way until it stops,* she thought. *I'll just stay this way forever,* she thought.

But forever had only just begun when feet scraped into her room. Nathaniel's footy pajamas made him look like one of Dr. Seuss's Sneetches — or was it a Who? Penelope couldn't remember — and gave his footsteps a sandpapery sound as they scratched the wood floor.

"What?" said Penelope into the pillow.

"Can I watch *The Smurfs* in here?"

"What's wrong with your TV?"

"Channel 7 has lines in it."

"I need to study for —" Penelope started to say when a door slammed down the hall. She lifted up her head and motioned for her brother to come in.

"Denise, cut me a break for once. Please. I'm barely off the airplane."

"You're barely off the airplane and you're barely back on. What else is new? And please don't expect me to feel sorry for you. You're off gallivanting in Europe while I'm home with the kids."

"Gallivanting! I —"

If her father was going to finish his sentence, Penelope didn't let him. "Close the door behind you," she instructed Nathaniel.

"My friend Matty's parents got divorced," clamored

Nathaniel as he shuffled into the room. "He's got *two* apartments, a cat *and* a dog, and he celebrates Christmas *twice*. Do you think Mommy and Daddy will get divorced?"

"Just 'cause they're fighting doesn't mean they'll get divorced," said Penelope, sitting up.

"We could have two apartments!" he yelped happily. "I could get Atari in one and ColecoVision in the other."

"Don't be dumb," scolded Penelope

"Sorry," mumbled Nathaniel. He'd picked up Penelope's bad habit of apologizing too much.

Somehow — with the door closed and the TV on — they still managed to hear Mrs. Schwartzbaum stomping down the hallway toward the kitchen. "I can't do this now, Herb!" she hollered. "I need some coffee. The week I've had! I'm so tired." Penelope hadn't heard those words in a while.

Channel 7 came in perfectly in Penelope's room. Nathaniel curled himself into a happy little red ball at the foot of her bed, and Penelope decided to do her homework. She hadn't even started studying for the big Algebra test. Mr. Bobkin had handed out review problems. You had to add, subtract, and multiply Xs and Ys, and solve word problems about a guy named Mario running next to a trout stream.

She sharpened her pencil and opened a pad of

graph paper. She wrote her name in the top right hand of the page, one letter in every box. P-E-N-E-L-O-P-E. Oops, the last "E" took up one and a half boxes! Penelope crumpled up the paper and started again.

The Smurfs turned to *Scooby Doo*, and Penelope struggled with Review Question #1. It was too hard. Maybe she'd do her Social Studies reading instead.

Scooby Doo turned to *Scrappy Doo*. Penelope could hear faint sounds coming from the kitchen. Had her parents made up? She tried to concentrate on the reading.

Scrappy Doo turned into an educational program, something about kids all over the world. Nathaniel watched a story about Eskimo kids who skinned blubber off of whales, then announced that he was starving. "I don't wanna go to the kitchen if they're fighting in there," he whined. "Will you get me a bagel, please? Or cereal. Special K with extra sugar and only a little milk! Please, Penelope, please!"

"Yeah, but you owe me," Penelope said, not admitting that she was starving, too.

Penelope wasn't usually an eavesdropper, and in Penthouse C she certainly didn't have to be. Sound traveled from one room to the next with ease, and her parents weren't exactly mumblers to begin with. But Penelope liked the sneaky feeling she got as she tiptoed down the hallway toward the voices in the kitchen. She lingered under the shadowy frame of the kitchen door and peered inside.

Her mother was standing at the counter. In front of her were piles of china plates and teacups. And then Penelope remembered: Her mother was having a tea today.

Fred Something was coming over.

Chapter Twelve

"It's just tragic," lamented Mrs. Schwartzbaum as she jabbed a stick of butter with a wooden spoon.

Mr. Schwartzbaum was sitting at the kitchen table, dangling a pen over the *New York Times* crossword puzzle.

"Herbert, don't you think it's just tragic?"

"Mmmmmm hmmmm."

"Herbert, what did I just say?" The wooden spoon had lodged itself in the butter, and Mrs. Schwartzbaum had to grip it with two hands to pull it out.

"Huh?"

"What did I say was tragic?"

"Uh, the deviled eggs you made are gloppy?"

"No, but I'm glad to know you think so." Mrs. Schwartzbaum grimaced.

"So what's tragic?" he asked, tugging at the ends of his mustache and frowning over the puzzle.

"This poor girl Cass who's coming over today, it's just tragic. She lost both her parents in a car crash in Sweden — or maybe it was Switzerland, I can't remember. So, she lives with Bea Levin. Technically, Bea's not even her grandmother. I guess she was the girlfriend of the father's father a zillion years ago — they never married, but she took the name."

Mrs. Schwartzbaum puzzled over that for a second. "Or something like that," she added.

"Mmmmmm hmmmmm," said Mr. Schwartzbaum.

"She's had the girl since she was eight. That's Nathaniel's age! Can you imagine? Our poor little Natty with no parents! Fred was telling me there's an aunt who helps out, too. You know who it is? That therapist who writes all those books? Doris? Doris Blume? She has a practice right here on West End. I see her at Zabar's sometimes. I guess I could have invited her also. But that might look grubby, right? Like I want her to come just because she's semifamous."

If Penelope was scared that her mother and Fred Something were having an affair, well then, the fact that her mother was throwing a tea for Fred Something when her father was home was a pretty good sign *they weren't*. After all, Monica Quartermaine would never have Rick Weber over when her husband, Alan, was home. But, *General Hospital* was a soap opera, and this was real life, and Penelope had to imagine there were some differences. If Tillie's parents were any indication, affairs really happened.

"Herb, do you think you could *not* do the crossword puzzle before company comes? No offense, but you're not very pleasant when you're frustrated."

"Just because you say 'no offense' doesn't mean what you say isn't offensive," Mr. Schwartzbaum replied. "And for your information, this relaxes me."

"I don't see how. All those tiny little words in all those tiny little boxes. It's enough to make a person dizzy."

"Well, I guess some people are puzzle people and some people —" He didn't bother finishing.

Penelope thought: *When I grow up, will I be a puzzle person?* Mr. Schwartzbaum was usually an alien figure to her, large and scary and distant, but watching his pencil hover expectantly over the half-done crossword, she had a cozy familiar feeling. She abridged her thought: *When I grow up, I hope I am a puzzle person.*

"Penelope had better be nice to this girl. She said some nonsense about signing a pledge not to talk to new kids. Adolescents can be so cruel. I won't allow her to be unkind in my house. I hope you're with me. I wonder if Stacy signed this silly pledge, too. Do you think Shirley Commack knows about it? I can't imagine she would allow for that kind of elitist behavior, what with her political inclinations. . . ."

"Right, right," said Herbert Schwartzbaum. "Well, you know how girls that age are. If Stacy jumped off the Brooklyn Bridge, Penelope would probably —"

It didn't matter that Mr. Schwartzbaum didn't finish his sentence. Penelope knew how it went. *Jump, too. If Stacy jumped off the Brooklyn Bridge, Penelope would probably jump, too.* She knew it was a popular phrase, she'd even heard people on TV shows say it — people who didn't live in New York City. But, as someone who lived in the city, who actually *saw* the Brooklyn Bridge from time to time, Penelope considered the phrase way too easy to imagine.

Stacy plummeting through the air, feet first, arms outstretched, blond curls scattered. Penelope somersaulting after her, as cabs honked, motors roared, and the East River gurgled below, ready to gobble them up.

The doorbell rang, and Mrs. Schwartzbaum had her hands full, so she screamed for Penelope to get it. Penelope had to run through the kitchen to do so. "Morning, kiddo!" greeted her father. She gave him a happy wave, pretending he hadn't just conjured up an image of her plunging to a brutal and untimely death.

It was Carlos with a platter of smoked salmon from Murray's Sturgeon Shop. He was followed by Jenny, who took over kitchen duties so Mrs. Schwartzbaum could freshen up.

Mrs. Schwartzbaum's rule of interior design was that there be no more than three colors per room, and that one of them always be black. Penelope, dressed for company in a hunter green cashmere sweater and a navy plaid kilt over cable-knit tights, was piling red cloth napkins on the glass coffee table in the black and white living room when the guests arrived. Mrs. Schwartzbaum had insisted Nathaniel dress up in a button-down shirt and flannel pants, and as he scurried down the hallway to greet the company — as Mrs.

Schwartzbaum had *also* instructed — his shirt magically untucked itself.

The first thing Penelope thought when she saw the famous art collector Bea Levin was that her face looked like a crumpled brown lunch bag. She was very tall and very suntanned — from a recent trip to Egypt, she explained, which also accounted for her large coin-shaped earrings and the gigantic turquoise scarab on a chain around her neck. She was the kind of woman who hugged people when she first met them, and with her face smushed in the folds of Bea's enormous blue velvet top, she missed the entrance of Fred Something.

By the time she unlodged herself from the old lady's grasp, Fred Something's back was to her, and standing before her — staring at her through one-eyed heart-shaped sunglasses — was the weird girl she'd met on the street. *The crazy person! The one who talked about making statements!* She was wearing the same exact outfit — the jacket covered in buttons, the corduroy baseball hat, the dirty sweatpants — the only difference was there was no Sylvia Hempel.

"Hi, Miss Marple!" she shouted as if Penelope was just the person she'd expected to see. "Remember me? That day? We were looking at the Moe Was Heres? I have a dog —"

Penelope cut the strange girl off. "I remember, it's just . . . ? My mom was saying you went to my school?"

She sounded like Pia Smith all of a sudden; every sentence was a question.

"I do," the girl answered plainly. "I started Elston this year. Seventh grade."

Penelope had the same eerie feeling she'd gotten the last time she'd met this weirdo, like a trick was being played on her.

"Bea doesn't let me wear this stuff to school," Cass offered as explanation. "This is my dog-walking outfit. Or my 'Go-visit-my-aunt-Doris-outfit.' Or my 'Walk-in-Central-Park-outfit.' I guess you could say it's my 'What-I-wear-when-I'm-not-in-school-outfit.' Don't worry, I wash it. It doesn't smell."

Penelope just stood there.

"You know you act dumb sometimes," Cass said.

Penelope was so frazzled by this girl's manner, she could barely respond. It was hard not to stutter, but speaking in one-word sentences made it easier. "What?" she said.

"I don't mean dumb as in stupid. I mean dumb as in dumb. As in not being able to talk. You're doing it on purpose, right? It's a good trick. It's a good way to get stuff out of people."

"Why would I want to get stuff out of people?"

"Well, if you were a detective, you'd want to, or a psychotherapist — like my aunt Doris. You know, if you had a job where you were trying to get people to start babbling. My theory is, the less one person talks, the more the other person wants to spill their guts."

"Case in point," interrupted Bea Levin, inserting herself in between the girls. "Cass, you've been monopolizing poor Penelope, and you haven't even met her parents. And how about taking off your hat and sunglasses? You do realize we're inside?" Coming from another adult mouth, this might have sounded scolding. But Bea had a comforting way about her.

Still, Cass scowled, begrudgingly removed her hat and glasses, and allowed herself to be escorted away. Which gave Penelope the opportunity to flee to the kitchen. It wasn't that she was *eager* to see Fred Something. *She'd sooner pretend he didn't exist. But that wasn't easy to do when he was live, in person, and in the next room.*

Penelope entered the kitchen, and there, standing over the counter talking to Jenny as she poured boiling water through a strainer of tea leaves, was Fred Something. Whenever Mrs. Schwartzbaum gushed about him, she mentioned how incredibly young he was. Staring up at this large man who had a mustache like her father's — only a tad wispier — and brown hair only slightly shorter than her own, and tiny wrinkles around the mouth and eyes, she thought, *Will I ever be so old that I think someone* his *age is young? Boy, my mother is old.*

Fred Something stared shyly at the floor when shaking her hand, like he'd lost something very small.

He acts like I caught him in the middle of something bad, thought Penelope, as Fred followed Jenny out of the kitchen and into the living room, where tea was being served.

"What? It's too boring in there for you?" Cass laughed upon entering the kitchen.

"I was gonna come in," answered Penelope, who wasn't quite sure how long she'd been sitting in the kitchen by herself.

"Yeah, well, I don't blame you. A lotta art talk. Your brother's pretty funny, though. He just sang a song about deviled eggs. Bea thinks he's like the next Cole Porter."

"Who's Cole Porter?"

"Some guy who sings Broadway show tunes. It's a compliment."

"Well, that's nice of your grandmother."

"She's not really my grandmother, you know. I call her that sometimes, but really she's just Bea."

"Sorry," said Penelope. "I mean Bea."

"You don't have to apologize."

"Sorry," said Penelope without thinking.

"You really have a problem with that, don't you?" It turned out having two Cass eyes staring at you was a lot more disconcerting than one, and Penelope almost wished Cass would put her one-eyed sunglasses back on. Not that anything was wrong with Cass's face. Underneath the glasses, the normalness of her features was almost shocking to Penelope. She had pale skin that looked a touch yellow under the overhead light, straight black hair cut in a sharp edge at the chin, and thin pink lips.

"It makes me mad when people say 'sorry' to me. For a whole year, that's all they said: I'm sorry about your parents. I'm sorry for your loss. I'm sorry. I'm sorry. I'm sorry. Bleah! It's enough to make you barf. 'Cause you know what they're really saying? I feel sorry for you. And that's the worst thing of all."

Penelope didn't think this sounded right, but she didn't think she could argue, either. Nothing like what had happened to Cass had ever happened to her.

"So how come I've never seen you in school?" she asked, still not sure Cass wasn't putting one over on her about going to Elston.

"I'm invisible."

"Yeah, right."

"Well, I don't know why. You tell me."

"Huh?"

"I don't know why you haven't seen me. I've seen you. You're always with that one girl, what's her name . . ."

"Stacy."

"Right, Stacy. She's in my Algebra class."

"Oh, yeah?" said Penelope. "She's never mentioned you."

Cass let out a wallop of a laugh. "Ba-ha! Like she would! I told you — I'm invisible. At least to all you people who think you're too good for us new kids."

The conversation was teetering on uncomfortable, so Penelope asked Cass if she wanted a Purple Cow. Cass said yes, even though she didn't know what one was. Penelope poured the grape soda over a scoop of vanilla ice cream, and the ingredients combined to make a beautiful violet foam in the lavender-tinted glasses Mrs. Schwartzbaum put out for company.

"So, what do you think of Fred?" Penelope asked because she couldn't think of anything else to say.

"He's nice," said Cass, sticking the tip of her tongue into the foam. "Ha!" She laughed when it rose up to her nose.

"You gotta wait a couple secs," giggled Penelope.

"Why did you ask about Fred?"

"I don't know. My mom spends a lot of time with him."

"What? That bothers you?"

Did this girl have ESP?

Before Penelope could answer, Cass let out a hoot. "Ooooh, it does! It bothers you! What? Do you think they're having an affair or something?"

These were the kinds of thoughts Penelope tried to forget! They were not the kinds of thoughts she spoke out loud. OR SCREAMED AT THE TOP OF HER LUNGS, for that matter.

"Wow!" yelped Cass, her small, pale hands colliding in a gleeful clap.

Suddenly, everything was going so fast! "Shhhhhh," Penelope hissed. "I didn't say that." Cass looked skeptical. "Okay, f-fine," stumbled Penelope. "It's just she talks about him a lot and my dad's never home and he gave her a present like this other couple I know who are having an affair."

"Who's that?"

"Uh, just these doctor friends of Stacy's mom's," lied Penelope. She might not have a handle on Cass's personality yet, but she was pretty sure she wasn't a *General Hospital* watcher.

"Well, there's only one way to find out the truth."

"What do you mean?"

"You gotta seek it out. That's what my aunt Doris always says. *'The truth is out there. You just gotta seek it.'* Follow them around. Catch them in the act."

This girl was insane. Who'd she think she was, Harriet the Spy? Penelope was *not* following her mother and Fred Something around. She'd get caught. She didn't know her mother's schedule. And, anyway, this was dumb. Why was she even thinking about this? Fred Something and her mother weren't having an affair, they weren't. What had made her talk to this girl? She felt dizzy.

"I'm not saying they're having an affair. I'm just saying that's the way to find out," declared Cass.

In a million trillion years this was nothing Penelope would ever do. But before she could put the topic to rest, Bea Levin entered the room. "Well, Ms. Cass, if you've guzzled down as much sugar as humanly possible, I think it's time to leave this poor family alone." Cass rolled her eyes at Penelope, finished the last of her drink, then hopped off the kitchen stool.

Bea gave Penelope another hug. "I'm so glad we got to do this," she told her. "I only wish Cass hadn't hogged you all afternoon. You seem terrifically interesting." She gripped Penelope's shoulders with her hands, and stared directly at her. "And what a fabulous friend you have in Jenny! You know, back in the prehistoric era, I went to Columbia for Art History." Bea looked wistful for a moment. "Seeing her just takes me back. Not that I ever looked like *that,* mind you, but, still . . ."

At Mrs. Schwartzbaum's request, Nathaniel brought the guests their coats. Bea's red cape was so heavy — it was a mix of shearling and mohair, a souvenir from Indonesia, Bea informed them — he practically had to drag it to her.

"Thank you, young sir," Bea Levin laughed, swooping the coat into her arms. "Do you know what you are?"

Nathaniel shook his head.

A big pain, thought Penelope.

"An original talent. And isn't that a superb thing to be?"

Mrs. Schwartzbaum liked to clean as soon as guests left, and when Penelope begged to "do it later," her mother gave her usual response: The longer they waited, the worse it would be.

Penelope and Jenny removed the white linen tablecloth from the kitchen table, and Mrs. Schwartzbaum inspected it for stains. She discovered a blob of chocolate near the left-hand corner (*clearly Nathaniel's doing,* thought Penelope), which she blotted with a mixture of ice water and bleach. "See, Penelope?" her mother demonstrated. "If you'd had it your way, we would have ignored this and the stain would be permanent."

They washed the cups and saucers and teapots by hand; they returned the china plates to their quilted zip-up protectors; Penelope wiped the glass coffee table with Windex while Jenny prepared a plate of leftover salmon sandwiches and miniature cookies for Carlos, and Mrs. Schwartzbaum buffed the leather sofas with a soft cloth.

When they were done, Mrs. Schwartzbaum swiped her hand across her forehead exultantly, surveyed their work with a tired smile, and pronounced it complete. "Excellent work, ladies," she proclaimed. "Like nobody was here."

This was a phrase Mrs. Schwartzbaum used on the rare occasion that the rooms in Penthouse C were suitably neat: *It's like nobody was here.* It would leave her lips with a proud nod of the head and a tired, happy gasp.

Penelope thought it was funny that her mother could be so very excited to have people over, and then so very relieved when not a trace of them remained.

Chapter Thirteen

The next morning, a note was delivered to Penelope. It said:

> Meet me on the bench outside the side
> entrance of the Guggenheim today at 2.
> Your mom and Fred are going to a lecture.
> If you want to seek the truth, you'll show up.
> If not, oh well.
>
> > Sincerely,
> > Cass
>
> P.S. Thanks for the purple cow.

Penelope had planned on studying for the Algebra test all day. She really had. She hadn't even considered meeting Cass. But at noon, when she heard the sounds of her mother preparing to go out — the shower, a blow-dryer, then humming (was her mother *really* humming?) — curiosity started to get the better of her.

She tried to resist it. She had work to do! If she didn't study, she was going to fail the Algebra test! She tried to do a word problem about a guy named Mario jogging along a trout stream. But every time Mario started his jog along the stream, she forgot about how many miles he went, and who was faster, him or the trout, and all she could think was, *Who's this stupid guy Mario? Who cares about trout? And why is my mother humming?*

She called Stacy. Whether she actually wanted to talk to her or if her fingers longed to perform their familiar dance on the number pad, Penelope wasn't sure. But she knew that if she heard Stacy's voice, she could get rid of the curiosity.

After three rings, Shirley Commack answered.

"Oh, hi, Pen — *crunch!* — how are you? — *crunch!* — good? — sorry, I'm eating potato chips." There was a rumpling of the bag. "I guess I don't have to tell you that. You know what I'm like on deadline. Anyway, Stacy's not here. Hasn't been all weekend. Somehow, don't ask me how, she resisted a fun weekend at home and opted for a glamorous sleepover at Vicki's house. You can call her there. She's probably salivating over their precious Park Avenue pad as we speak. *Crunch!*"

Shirley Commack hung up before Penelope could ask for Vicki's number. She'd have to get it off the class list. But where was that? She was searching her room when she heard the noises: the clipping of high heels, the jangle of her mother's keys, doors closing — first the coat closet door, then the front door. Penelope abandoned her search for the seventh-grade class list and Vicki's number. Instead, she threw a sweatshirt over her head, pulled on her Levi's, and shoved her feet into her Tretorns without lacing them up. She'd get them in the elevator. She grabbed her coat. It was 1:35, and if she ran to the bus, she might still make it.

"What mischief are you up to today, Miss Penelope?" asked Carlos as she tore across the lobby. Penelope knew he was joking — she'd be the last person to do anything Carlos considered remotely bad — but as he waggled his finger at her as if to say "I'm onto you," she felt a surge of energy go through her and she ran to the crosstown bus in record time, not even stopping to search for Moes.

"You showed up," said Cass. She was sitting on the stone bench doing Fundamental Languages homework. "I'm impressed."

Penelope ignored this. She was more interested in Cass's outfit. Apparently her sunglasses and jacket with all the buttons were too conspicuous for detective work, so she was dressed like a normal girl in gray corduroys so brand-new they were still creased down the fronts, a black-and-yellow-striped rugby shirt, a down vest over a Levi's jeans jacket, and white Stan Smith Adidas sneakers. "Is that how you dress for school?" Penelope asked.

"Yeah," answered Cass solemnly.

"You look good."

"Of course you'd think that."

"I like your shirt."

"Yeah, well, you can have it, if you want. I feel like a bumblebee in it." She scrunched her face up and gnarled her fingers into tiny antennae. *"Bzzzzzzzzzz . . . ,"* she whispered in Penelope's ear. *"Bzzzzzzzzzzzzz."* Penelope swatted Cass away, and once again had the feeling she was in the company of a crazy person.

Cass had already scouted out the scene at the Guggenheim, so she knew exactly where they should go. "It should be prime viewing and hiding here," she whispered, directing Penelope down a hallway. "We can watch them on line to get into the lecture without being seen."

A professor from France was giving the lecture. The subject was "Modern Sculpture and Madness in Montmartre." *Whatever that means,* thought Penelope. She watched the line form. There were old couples, a woman with Albert Einstein hair, a red-bearded guy with an eye patch . . .

"Bzzzzzzzz," went Cass in her ear.

"Stop that," snapped Penelope.

"I'm trying to tell you something," urged Cass. "Look." At the end of the line, half-hidden by a large man in a NY Jets jacket, were Mrs. Schwartzbaum and Fred Something. It was funny: Mrs. Schwartzbaum talked so loudly at home, but Penelope couldn't hear a word she was saying now. She and Fred stood so close together, they reminded Penelope of the stuffed monkeys Ivy gave Nathaniel for his eighth birthday. The monkeys were attached at the cheek and locked in a permanent embrace. "Stop breathing so loud," hissed Cass through gritted teeth. "You're louder than Sylvia Hempel."

Penelope had heard people on television say they "could feel their hearts beating," but she hadn't known what they'd meant until now, when her heart felt like it could thump right out of her chest. She ground her sneakers into the floor. Clutching the sleeve of Cass's jacket — she hadn't meant to! It just happened — she watched Fred and Mrs. Schwartzbaum glide by. They disappeared into the lecture hall.

"Drinks are on you!" announced Cass once the hallway was empty.

"What?" asked Penelope, who was still a little shaken up.

"I'm doing you a favor. You buy the drinks."

Penelope reached into her jeans pocket. She'd left the house without preparation, and all she had on her were her bus pass and three crumpled-up dollar bills.

Cass marched to the Guggenheim coffee shop, where they waited at a table, sipping Cokes with ice. Cass went back to her F. L. homework, and Penelope felt dumb for not having brought the Algebra review problems with her. She'd only made it through two so far, and she wasn't positive she'd gotten either right. She stared out the window thinking about *General*

Hospital and Rick and Monica and what she'd wear tomorrow.

Had Cass really meant it when she said she'd give her that rugby shirt? Wouldn't it go well with her white Levi's? But that was a dumb thing to think about! If Penelope took the shirt, that would mean they were friends. And they *weren't* friends. They were just doing this one weird thing together today.

"Penelope? What are you doing here?" Just as Penelope was thinking *Tomorrow will be back to normal,* she heard the familiar voice. She looked up to see Tillie Warner standing over the table. "That's so weird to run into you here! My mom makes me come to museums all the time, and I *never* run into friends from school." She motioned to a table where Cherry Warner sat hunched over a cup of coffee.

"She says it's her way to escape her rotten life," whispered Tillie. "She's having a bad weekend. My dad came to pick up his stuff. And he brought Rochelle. To our house! Can you believe it?"

Tillie's mother's bad weekend showed in Tillie's cheeks, which were speckled with measlelike spots. "I know, I know," Tillie blathered when she saw where Penelope's eyes had landed. "My face is an eczema explosion." She reached to cover the spots with her hands. Penelope averted her eyes. Tillie's hands didn't look so good, either. They looked dry and scaly.

"It gives you character," declared a bold voice from the other side of the table.

Penelope had almost forgotten about Cass.

Tillie's eyes shifted Cass's way, and Penelope watched miserably as Tillie put it all together. "Hey," Tillie declared with stunned realization, "I know you!"

"I'm Cass. I'm in your English class."

"Right! I'm Tillie."

Cass nodded. Apparently, she knew that already.

"You're new, right?" Tillie asked. When Cass shook her head yes, Tillie's eyebrows arched upward as did the corners of her mouth.

"I liked the stuff you said about *The Old Man and the Sea*," Cass told Tillie. "You made it actually seem like a good book. I mean, before that class I was thinking: Who cares about an old man or the sea?"

Penelope wondered if the desire to evaporate could actually make her evaporate.

"Well, Ms. Betz can make anything boring, if you ask me. *Julius Caesar* is this really exciting play, right? In her class, it's a giant yawn. And doesn't it seem to last forever, that class? Every time I look at the clock, I think an hour has gone by — but it's five minutes!"

"Speaking of clocks," said Cass, glancing at her watch, then looking up at Penelope. "We should go." The lecture was about to let out.

Penelope nodded meekly.

She wanted nothing more than to avoid being confronted by Tillie. She wanted nothing more than to skulk out of there. To pretend this had never happened! She protested when Cass said she was going to throw away their Coke cups. "Let's just go," she muttered.

"I'm not going to just *leave* them here for someone else to clean up," Cass scolded. "We still have a minute."

"Hey," whooped Tillie once they were alone. "You're hanging out with a new kid! Ha! Guess you want to cross your name off The Pledge, too!" If Penelope was going to respond, she didn't have time. Cass was back. Good-bye was all there was time to say.

Penelope and Cass resumed their positions and watched as Fred Something and Mrs. Schwartzbaum sauntered out of the lecture, out the museum door, and onto Fifth Avenue. The air was brittle, but Mrs. Schwartzbaum — who usually complained about the cold — didn't seem to mind. She grinned as she pulled her silk scarf tighter around her head, watching admiringly as Fred Something hailed a cab. Even Penelope had to admit that, with his arm outstretched, Fred Something looked pretty commanding — almost as commanding as Carlos, and he was a professional cab hailer.

A shiny Checker cab arrived, and Fred Something opened the yellow door for Mrs. Schwartzbaum, then leaned his own tall body in. Penelope couldn't see what he was doing. Was he getting in? Saying something mushy? Giving her mother a kiss?

She'd never know. Moments later, the cab was whizzing down Fifth Avenue and Fred Something was loping his way across the street and into the park.

Penelope and Cass followed Fred Something down a winding path, past the Alice statue, past the model boat pond. They watched him buy a coffee at the refreshment stand. Then they trailed him as he exited the park at Seventy-second street. He proceeded to Madison Avenue where he window shopped — for the most boring things imaginable: ties, leather address books, art posters. He spent a full twenty minutes gazing at an antique typewriter. They followed him until Sixty-sixth street, until Cass said she had to go. "I'd say chances of an affair are fifty-fifty," she said, brusquely, before turning east, toward her house. "It could go either way."

That night Penelope had the dream about Stacy and the rope ladder, only this time, Tillie was standing at the edge of the pit, peering in at Penelope and laughing.

Chapter Fourteen

"You don't understand, I didn't study at all. I'm totally going to fail!" cried a distressed Annabella Blumberg. She stomped her foot, and her brown suede clog made an angry clap on the cafeteria's linoleum floor.

It was the morning of the Algebra test, and girls from Bobkin's three Algebra sections huddled around a long table littered with orange juice cartons and corn muffin wrappers, crumpled-up pieces of graph paper, and pencil stubs. "Oh, Annabella, don't worry, you're not going to fail," consoled Pia, who wasn't studying but was busily making mysterious checkmarks on her clipboard.

"Yeah, I'm the one who's *really* going to fail!" blustered Stacy, wiping a frustrated tear from her eye.

Vicki's head bobbed sadly in agreement.

Here was something Penelope noticed: People who failed tests, who *actually* failed tests, never made a big deal about it. But the ones who sobbed and whined and worked themselves into a lather always did fine. It was contagious. One girl would say: "I'm going to fail." Then another girl would say: "No, *I'm* going to fail." And it went on and on like that until the test happened, and *nobody* failed.

Except Penelope, that is.

She'd come home after her trip to the Guggenheim with Cass and she'd *tried* to study, she really had, but there'd been too much to think about: Tillie and The Pledge, Mrs. Schwartzbaum and Fred Something, Cass and what she would do if she ran into her in the halls at school.

It turned out she didn't have to worry about Tillie. Because she didn't come to school that Monday. Or Tuesday or Wednesday. "She says it's her asthma," whispered Vicki in her most top-secret voice to anyone who would listen. "But if you ask me, it's her mom. I heard from my dad, who's friends with Tillie's dad, that Cherry Warner's certifiable."

"What does 'certifiable' mean?" Penelope asked. She'd heard divorces were complicated, and maybe being certifiable was one of the steps between separation and divorce.

"It's a way of saying she's crazy," Vicki said, as if this were the most obvious thing on earth. "Like she should go to a mental institution."

"Oh," said Penelope. Cherry Warner hadn't looked crazy when she and Cass had seen her at the Guggenheim, but she couldn't bring that up.

Speaking of Cass, it turned out Penelope didn't have to worry about running into her in the halls. Because wherever Penelope was, Cass wasn't. They didn't have homeroom together. They didn't have classes together. Penelope never saw her in gym or at lunch. Still,

Penelope walked with her head hanging downward, like she was searching for Moe Was Heres on West End Avenue. Just in case.

Without Tillie blocking her view, Penelope had a much better view of Dr. Alvin during homeroom. She was wearing a beige sweater, which gave her puckered face a sallow look. Underneath each eye was a leathery gray purse of tired skin.

"It has come to my attention," grumbled Dr. Alvin through gritted teeth, "that some kind of pledge has been circulating the seventh grade. Something about segregating the new kids from the old. What do you people think this is? Kindergarten?"

The class was silent. Dr. Alvin continued. "I'm going to give you an option," she told them. "You can confess, tell me you signed The Pledge, explain the errors of your ways, and there will be no punishment. Or you can take a risk, gamble on whether this pledge will make its way to the administration. If it does and I see your name, and you haven't confessed, I promise the consequences will be much worse."

Penelope spent extra time packing her backpack after class, lagging to see if anyone confessed to Dr. Alvin. When no one did, she sped out of the classroom and toward the library. "Did you need to talk to me about anything, Penelope?" Dr. Alvin called out to her. Penelope pretended like she didn't hear her.

She had a free period before the Algebra test and she settled in a corner by the back of the library, opened her textbook, and pulled out her review questions. *Study*, she told herself. *Study*.

If X times Y = Z, then what would Tillie do when she heard about Dr. Alvin and The Pledge? Would she turn herself in? Would Stacy? Would Vicki? They would if it affected their college records. Would it? And how would Dr. Alvin ever get her hands on The Pledge? Could she steal Pia's clipboard? Could she? Would a teacher do that?

Why hadn't Penelope studied? *Study*, she commanded herself. *Study! You have to study! It's pathetic, it's pitiful!* Why hadn't she studied?

Could a stomach hiccup? Because if it could, that's what Penelope's was doing. She was so hungry. Starving, in fact. Why, she'd never felt this starving in her entire life. She was going to have to eat something.

She could go to the vending machine. Get a 3 Musketeers bar, that would be just the thing. Then she could study.

Stacy and Vicki had already taken their Algebra test, and they were giddy with the relief of having it over with. "I have to go. I have an Algebra test," Penelope announced when she saw them.

"Don't say *hi* or anything," Stacy teased.

"Yeah, your royal rudeness." Vicki laughed.

"Sorry," murmured Penelope. She punched D4 for 3 Musketeers.

"Did your homeroom teacher give you a lecture about The Pledge?" asked Vicki. "What a joke. Like they'll ever get the copy of it. Pia's got the only one." *Flump* went the 3 Musketeers as it hit the metal bottom of the machine.

"Whoever confesses is moronic. There's no point. *Nothing's* going to happen to us."

On the way back to the library, Penelope ate the chocolate bar. It was gone in four swift chomps, and before she was pushing open the library's heavy wood door, the wrapper was crumpled up in her front jeans pocket.

Back in the library. Ten more minutes. She could memorize three equations in that time, she was sure she could. *If X times Y equals Z, then Z divided by Y equals X.* She placed her palm over the equation and tried to recite it back silently in her head. *If X times Y equals Z, then Z divided by Y equals X.* Or was it *If X times Y equals Z, then Z divided by X equals Y*?

The clock stared at her. Two minutes to go. Two minutes! How had she wasted eight whole minutes? She'd wasted the free period! She couldn't even re-member eating the chocolate bar! It hadn't been worth eating. If she hadn't gone to get it, she wouldn't have had to talk to Vicki and Stacy. Because they just made her feel stupid! Stupider!

One minute. She put her Algebra textbook and her notebook in her backpack, her head brimming with Xs and Ys and Zs and guys named Mario, trout, streams, her mother, Fred Something, Tillie, Stacy, Vicki . . . She ran out of the library, blasted out of the building, and cut across the field, and somewhere between the bleachers and Gritzfield Hall, fell into a daze. It was like the daze that overcame her in Algebra sometimes, but even more intense. It was the stuffed-in-the-head feeling you got when you had a cold, only without the cold.

I can't feel this way. Not now! I don't have time. I can't afford it. I have to concentrate.

But by the time she got to Bobkin's class, she had a head full of mayonnaise. And even worse, she'd lost her pencil. She had to borrow one from Ben. It was red, and in gold lettering said: LUTKIN, SCHWARTZ, AND WHITE.

Question #1. Not so hard. Question #2. Not so bad, either. Question #3. She didn't even understand it.

Lutkin, Schwartz, and White. Lutkin, Schwartz, and White.

Skipped Question #4. Would come back to it later. Tried #5. Got through half. Filled in an answer for #6. Maybe he'd give points for trying. Went back to #3. Ack, still didn't understand.

Lutkin, Schwartz, and White. Lutkin, Schwartz, and White.

"Fifteen minutes!" shouted Bobkin.

There was some new graffiti on the desk: **LIFE SUX**,

someone had written. **AND THEN YOU DIE**, someone else had added. **LAURA K. = FUNNIEST SENIOR** was scratched inside a big red heart. **IGNORANCE IS BLISS** was in giant green bubble letters.

Ack! Why am I reading graffiti?

"Ten minutes!" shouted Bobkin.

Then, Penelope was scribbling numbers that weren't in equations, and subtracting Xs from problems that had only Zs and Ys.

"Pencils down!" the teacher shouted.

Penelope handed the pencil back to Ben, who told her to keep it. It was from his dad's law firm and he had a million. Woozily, she slipped the pencil into the front pouch of her backpack. "Hey," Ben said. "That test was hard, but are you okay? You look kinda weird."

She didn't answer.

"Oh, I get it. You don't talk to me anymore. See I noticed that, but I thought you were just shy. Now I know you're a Pledge person. Too great to talk to new kids? Well, I never would have figured you for a snot like that, but fine, be that way."

"I did terribly. No way you did as badly as I did," contended Stacy. They were on the school bus going home. The window wouldn't shut all the way, and Penelope zipped her blue sweatshirt high around her neck. "I failed. I just know I did."

Secretly, Stacy had to know she hadn't, but she sure looked like she believed it. Her lip jutted out, and her eyelids drooped, and she blinked super slowly. Penelope thought maybe somewhere Stacy really thought she'd gotten an F. She almost felt bad for her, but only for a second.

She could have countered with: "Yeah, well, I really failed. I left out the last four questions. I scribbled whatever came into my head." It might have felt good to shock Stacy — she might have even felt proud, having won the battle of *"Who can really fail?"*

But all she said was: "I'm sure you did fine."

"Hey, space cadet!" Stacy shouted, when five minutes had gone by and they hadn't exchanged a word. "I forgot to tell you that Vicki and I figured out who's writing the nasty stuff about The Pledge. You're not gonna believe it and you have to not tell anyone till Vicki finds out for sure. Are you ready?"

Penelope just stared out the window.

"Yoo hoo. I said, 'Are you ready?'"

Penelope stayed blank.

"Seriously, you don't want to know? Well, fine, then, I won't tell you." She folded her arms around her chest in exasperation. "I guess you're being smart. If you don't know, there's no risk of your telling anyone. What's that expression? 'Ignorance is bliss'? Still, I'm surprised you're being so disciplined. It's not like you. Oh, hey, my mom said you called Saturday night. She told you I was at Vicki's, right? Why didn't you call me there?"

Penelope didn't answer. The familiar words were floating through her brain, as if they were spelled out on a banner attached to the tail of an airplane half-hidden by clouds: *We don't match.*

"Hey, how many word problems were on your test? I bet there weren't half as many as on ours. You know, Bobkin is supposed to be the hardest Algebra teacher ever to be at Elston Prep. Just my luck, right?"

Penelope said nothing. She didn't remember how many word problems they'd had. She could barely remember the test at all. If she could, she might recall that just before time was up, she'd put down her pencil, taken a ballpoint pen from her pocket, and then, in tiny blue block letters, written on the desk: **PENELOPE B. SCHWARTZBAUM WAS HERE.**

"God, Penelope! Are you in a coma or what?"

Chapter Fifteen

"BLT, you gotta be
The sammy for me
Made by Jenny!

I'll eat you with my feet
My toes and with my nose
The way you crunch

I gotta hunch
You'll be my breakfast, dinner,
and my lunch
For eternity!"

Ever since Bea Levin had called Nathaniel talented, he'd been on a singing rampage. "Do you think you could shut up this century?" asked Penelope, who was doing her Fundamental Languages homework. They'd recently switched to French.

"You're just jealous 'cause I'm the next Dole Quarter," spat Nathaniel, dipping the last bite of his BLT into a pool of ketchup and chomping.

"You mean Dole PORTER, dope."

Jenny waited for Nathaniel to stop chewing, then removed the dirty plates from the table. "I believe you both mean Cole Porter. Nathaniel, wipe your mouth. All that ketchup makes you look like a vampire with a big, bloody mouth."

"AHHHHHHHHHHH!" Nathaniel yelled, opening his mouth to reveal mushed-up bacon and ketchup. "I've got fangs!"

"Uch," growled Penelope. "You are gross."

"I'm a talent!" shouted Nathaniel.

"On what planet?" asked Penelope.

"This planet! My planet! Planet Nathaniel!"

Jenny returned to the table with mugs of hot chocolate and a bag of marshmallows. "On Planet Nathaniel they wipe their dirty faces before getting hot chocolate." She handed him a wet paper towel and waited for him to slosh it across his mouth.

"Ooh, hot!" he yelped, putting his lips to the mug.

"Duh," said Penelope. "You have to wait a minute."

"Blow on it," suggested Jenny.

Instead, Nathaniel sang:

"Count Chocula
 I'd like to talk to ya
 I got ketchup on me
 Can't ya see"

"Jenny, do you think I'm the next Cole Quarter?"

"If you wanna be, Natty. Personally, I'd rather you be the next Elvis Costello. Want me to put him on while you eat your dessert?" She sliced them each a piece of pound cake, and put the tape on. Penelope was getting better at understanding the words, but she still didn't know what they meant.

"What's he singing about?" she asked Jenny.

"Honestly, I'm not always sure. Lots of different stuff. It's like a puzzle, trying to figure him out. Like a good book, you know?"

Penelope wasn't sure she did. On the record, Elvis Costello sang: "Isn't this the greatest thing? Isn't this the greatest thing?"

"What's the greatest thing?"

"I think he's talking about marriage."

"Marriage is the greatest thing?"

"He's being sarcastic, but I think that's maybe what he means, yeah."

"And what does he mean when he says 'punch the clock'?" As Penelope asked this, her eyes strayed toward the Sunburst Clock Fred Something had given her mother.

"I think it's a reference to having a job where you have to 'punch in.' You put a little card in a machine so it can record your hours."

"Like Fred Flintstone does!" shouted Nathaniel.

"Yes, exactly. And jobs you have to punch in for aren't always the most exciting. But he's saying it's okay, because he's in love and that's the greatest thing." Jenny looked thoughtful for a moment. "Either that, or punching the clock is a metaphor. Do you know what a metaphor is?"

Penelope nodded, even though she didn't know what a metaphor was.

"Well, maybe punching the clock is a metaphor for how relationships can go stale, and how sometimes you're just sleepwalking through them."

They drank second cups of hot chocolate and listened to the rest of side one without talking.

"My belly's full of marshmallow, playing Elvis Costello," crooned Nathaniel when it was over.

Later that evening, Cass called on the phone. Penelope knew it was Cass the second she picked up, because she could hear Sylvia Hempel barking in the background. Cass announced that she had a tip.

"A tip" sounded like detective lingo, and Penelope accused Cass of thinking she was Harriet the Spy. Immediately after saying it, she felt dumb. Cass talked about books for adults like Agatha Christie's and here she was bringing up a book Nathaniel would be reading in the fourth grade.

"First of all, we're being detectives, not spies. Second of all, you act like being Harriet the Spy would be a bad thing. That's, like, the greatest book of all time. I promise we're not going to read anything better in high school. Maybe as good, but not better. Fourth of all . . . or was I at third of all?"

Penelope told her she'd been at third of all, but Cass had forgotten what she was going to say. "So where do you go at school?" Penelope asked her.

That got a hoot out of Cass. "What do you care? You wouldn't hang out with me. I heard about The Pledge in homeroom."

Penelope tried to sound as offended as possible. "How do you know I signed The Pledge?" she asked.

"Ha!" said Cass, as if that said it all.

"You can't know for sure," said Penelope in an attempt to sound mysterious.

Cass ignored her. "Hey, what's that music in the background?" she asked. "It sounds pretty cool."

"Some guy named Elvis Costello," said Penelope, who could hear a key in the door. Her mother was home. "I gotta go," she told Cass.

"Hey!" shouted Cass. "I never told you why I was calling. I never told you the tip. So, Bea doesn't like to gossip, but that doesn't mean she can stop people from telling her stuff. Anyway, this artist who Fred Something works with told her that Fred is — get this — 'embarking on a new affair.' And guess what? Bea's friend called the woman 'Fred's age-inappropriate paramour.'"

Penelope didn't know what that meant.

"That it's your mother!" shouted Cass. "I mean, what? He's twenty-nine and she's, like, forty? Well, that's a whole lot older. Sounds 'age inappropriate' to me!"

Penelope thought for the rest of the night about what Cass said. Especially as she listened to her mother talk about the charity event she and Fred Something were planning together and how fabulous it was going to be, but how much work it was going to take, and how she wasn't going to be home a lot, but thankfully Jenny could do more hours. She was counting on Penelope to mind Jenny and to keep an eye on Nathaniel herself. He was so little and this was especially unfair to him, not having his parents around enough. It just broke her heart.

And then Mr. Schwartzbaum came home, but he went straight to his bedroom because he was taking the red-eye to California, a flight that went overnight, en route to Singapore. He'd be leaving in a matter of hours.

"Red-eye? You didn't tell me you were taking the red-eye!" complained Mrs. Schwartzbaum as she followed him to the bedroom. She slammed the door behind her, and they continued to argue while he packed.

THE NO NEWKS NEWKSLETTER

BY: THE NEWKLEAR POWERS THAT BE

IF YOU ARE READING THIS, THAT MEANS YOU DIDN'T GIVE IN AND TELL YOUR HOMEROOM TEACHER ABOUT US. CONGRATS!!!!!!!

S.C.'s STYLE GUIDE

COLORS THAT YOU THOUGHT DIDN'T MATCH, BUT DO: PINK AND MAROON

COLORS THAT *STILL* DON'T MATCH: RED AND ORANGE

THINGS NOT TO DO: DON'T TUCK IN YOUR SHIRT.

DON'T WEAR YOUR HAIR IN A MIDDLE PART.

DON'T WEAR PIGTAILS UNLESS YOU ARE CUTE, AND IF YOU ARE CUTE, YOU KNOW IT! (HI, V.F.!).

FASHION POLL
(SUBMIT RESPONSES TO P.S.!)

WHAT DO YOU LIKE BETTER? POLO OR LACOSTE (circle one).

WHICH TEAM HAS A CUTER UNI-FORM? FIELD HOCKEY OR SOCCER (circle one).

WHAT ARE YOU WEARING TO A.B.'S BAT MITZVAH?
(Keep answer under a paragraph.)

NOTE: IF YOU WROTE RED GUNNE SAX DRESS WITH HIGH HEELS, THINK AGAIN. THAT IS WHAT *SHE* IS WEARING AND IT WOULD BE *VERY RUDE* TO WEAR THE SAME THING. THIS IS IMPORTANT!!!!!!!!!!!!

WARNING

TO THE PERSON WRITING ABOUT US ON THE WALLS: WE'RE ONTO YOU.

IF YOU'RE READING THIS YOU DON'T DESERVE TO BE.

CONSIDER YOURSELF WARNED.

SIGNED, **P.S.**

COLLEGE UPDATE BY L.L.
LUCKY VICKI FELD IS A LEGACY KID. AT DARTMOUTH! (IVY LEAGUE.) HER GRANDPA AND DAD WENT THERE. WITH A *B* AVERAGE SHE'LL GET IN EARLY!

♥♥♥♥♥♥♥♥♥♥♥♥♥♥

GOSSIP ITEM

NOTE: THERE IS ONE NON-NO NEWKer WHO IS OKAY 2 TALK 2. THAT'S BECAUSE HE WENT TO CAMP WITH ANNABELLA. CAN YOU GUESS WHO IT IS?????????

♠♠♠♠♠♠♠♠♠♠♠♠♠

Chapter Sixteen

November turned to December, and the winds whipped and snarled along West End Avenue. Seventh graders retired their down vests for ski jackets, their cashmere sweaters for ragg wool ones ordered over the phone from L.L. Bean.

With Carlos's encouragement, Penelope and Nathaniel stopped waiting for the school bus on the sidewalk and moved inside. They sank into the lobby's hulking brown leather couch, huddled in their new down coats, and watched the morning's activities: The old lady from the fifteenth floor — a famous poet, according to Carlos — returning from her morning walk, her long, woolly hair held captive by her coat's giant hood; Mr. Pearl in his striped suit waddling off the elevator, a thermos of coffee in one hand, the *New York Times* in the other, humming a Broadway show tune.

Carlos wore a black wool coat with gold buttons, since he spent so much time outside hailing cabs for tenants in the building. His cheeks went from red-from-cold to red-from-heat, and he kept a stack of white ironed handkerchiefs in his coat pocket to blot his perpetually running nose.

After two weeks of absence, Tillie Warner returned

to Elston Prep, still wheezing, but looking slightly less measly than she had the day Penelope saw her at the Guggenheim. She had a brand-new haircut, so short that it was impossible to pull at. The back and sides were soft yet bristly like the fur on an orange tabby cat, and on the top of her head was a giant puff that reminded Penelope of a squirrel's tail.

"I thought you were sick, Tillie," remarked Stacy on Tillie's first morning back. They'd taken to hanging out in the cafeteria before homeroom.

"I was," Tillie told her. "I had horrible asthma." Tillie took a pink inhaler from her pocket and waved it in the air as proof.

"But you had time to go to La Coupe?" Stacy asked with a purposeful sip of coffee. It was a new habit she and Vicki had adopted, drinking coffee with half-and-half and Sweet'n Low in the morning. They served it in the cafeteria, much to the chagrin of Shirley Commack, who was threatening to call and protest.

"Actually, the guy from La Coupe came to us," said Tillie. "My mom didn't want to leave the house, you know, 'cause . . ." Her nervous hands — less scaly but still dry — uncoiled the metal spiral of her Earth Science notebook as she talked. By the time she was done, the metal stuck straight out — like a weapon.

"Well, I think your hair looks good," Penelope said, because no one else had.

"And it's practical," added Stacy. "You know, you can't pull on it."

Penelope wondered if she'd intended for that to come out as mean as it had.

"Nice earrings, Stace!" giggled Annabella Blumberg, taking a seat between Stacy and Vicki on the bench outside the cafeteria.

"Nice earrings, Annabella!" giggled Stacy.

Penelope wasn't sure how it had happened, but the fight about the feather earrings had become a joke between Annabella and Stacy. An inside joke. They said it every time they saw each other in the halls, and it never ceased to crack either of them up.

When someone who didn't know the joke asked what they were talking about, one of them would answer: "Inside joke, you wouldn't get it." Or: "It's just a dumb private joke, not worth getting into." Then they'd laugh some more.

"Did you hear about Tillie Warner?" interrupted Pia, who didn't like it when anybody other than she had anything *inside* or *private* with Annabella.

And, indeed they had. Word of Tillie's confession to Dr. Alvin about signing The Pledge — the first of any No-Newker — had spread through the grade by lunch period. Stacy and Vicki begged Penelope to relay any and all details of the confession — she was in Tillie's homeroom, after all — but she didn't know any.

Stacy wanted to know why Penelope hadn't waited outside homeroom for Tillie while she was talking to Dr. Alvin.

"Yeah," Vicki added, if not slightly suspiciously. Wasn't Penelope even a little curious as to what Tillie and the teacher were talking about? Could it be, they asked, that Penelope already knew what Tillie was going to do?

They interpreted the confusion on Penelope's face as ignorance.

"It's a question of character, if you ask me," said Pia. Not that anyone *had* asked her. "Tillie's a bad friend."

Vicki jumped in. Well, how did everyone think it made *her* feel? Tillie had been her best friend for four years, which was shorter than Stacy and Penelope but longer than Annabella and Pia.

They looked at her consolingly. Stacy put her arm around Vicki's shoulder. "I think this proves it," she said softly.

"Proves what?" scowled Pia, who didn't like feeling in the dark.

"It's obvious," retorted Stacy. Penelope noticed that the nicer Annabella was to Stacy, the more smug Stacy felt she could be to Pia.

"Okay, maybe I'm dense, but I don't get it," said Annabella. "What does it prove?"

"Well, I could be wrong, but . . ." Stacy was clearly

enjoying having all eyes on her, and she prolonged the moment accordingly. "Remember this is just a theory," she told them. "I don't know this for a fact, but —"

Annabella stamped the floor impatiently.

"Okay, I hate to say it," said Stacy. Now she was talking faster than her usual clipped pace. "But Tillie was the one writing the graffiti on the walls." She surveyed the shocked faces surrounding her and grinned proudly at the power of her words.

Penelope thought: *When people start sentences with "I hate to say it, but," they don't mean it. They should really say, "I'm so excited to say what I'm about to say."*

"I thought it was Tillie!" clapped Pia. "She was one of my suspects!"

Pia and Annabella formed a two-girl-huddle while the rest of them watched. Penelope caught words like "plans" and "punishment." And then Lillian Lang and a couple of other No-Newkers appeared, and Pia told them she'd call them tonight, they'd need to be prepped, they knew who was writing on the walls, it was Tillie, and they were going to do something about it.

Stacy didn't appear to regret her announcement, but right after the five-minute bell clanged and just before the group dispersed, Vicki called for everyone's attention. "Maybe Tillie's acting like such a weirdo," she suggested haltingly, "because her mom's cuckoo and her parents are getting divorced."

There were a couple of murmurs, and then Annabella replied flippantly, "Oh, everyone's parents get divorced. I mean, not mine, but everyone else's."

"Yeah," Pia chimed in. "It's no excuse to write on the walls. She wrote mean stuff about No Newks, which means she wrote mean stuff about you," she reminded her. "About all of us!"

Vicki acquiesced easily, and Penelope wondered whether she'd stuck up for Tillie more out of habit than conviction. With her head resting on Stacy's shoulder, Vicki looked more than happy to be the one on the receiving end of pity this time.

Penelope had been completely silent during these revelations. She'd thought about saying something in Tillie's defense, but Pia's last words had served as a rallying cry, and with two minutes until class, there was no hope of her formulating something to say.

She consoled herself on the walk to English class, thinking, *Pia is right. The person who wrote on the walls is mean. She's a liar. She's crazy. And she's not very brave at all.*

That afternoon, a new piece of writing appeared on the back of the bathroom door in the Solden Science Center. Pia studied it, but couldn't decipher if it was intended for the No Newkers, as it was a little more cryptic than the others had been.

It said:

If X × Z = Y, then
A Follower of a Follower = a Nobody

The one girl who would have understood its true meaning, Tillie, left school early that day because she had a doctor's appointment. She'd see it eventually — but it would be too late.

Chapter Seventeen

Tillie's newly visible neck and ears looked vulnerable when the girls surrounded her.

"Admit it, Tillie," ordered Annabella.

"Admit it, Tillie," echoed Pia.

"I can't believe you, Tillie!" charged Vicki.

"Just say you did it," commanded Stacy.

They stood in the middle of the football field, which had lost its lush greenness to winter and was now the color of a Triscuit. As the circle around her tightened — Pia, Annabella, Vicki, Stacy, Penelope, along with Lillian Lang and Annie Reed — the yellow scarf around Tillie's neck seemed to miraculously unwind itself. It was as if Pia, with her fashion industry expertise — her dad did own a mall! — had instructed the garment to leave poor Tillie as unprotected as possible.

"Admit it, Tillie. Admit it, Tillie. Admit it, Tillie."

Penelope thought, *If I mouth the words, but don't say them, does it count?*

"Admit it, Tillie. Admit it, Tillie. Admit it, Tillie."

Tillie seemed to have expected this. "What do you want me to admit? That I told Dr. Alvin I signed The Pledge?"

"You can start with that," said Pia.

"Fine," huffed Tillie. "I did. Big deal. I would have done it sooner if I hadn't been out of school. You know, if my mom —"

There were several groans from the crowd.

"Don't try to turn this into a pity party, Tillie." It was Vicki who spoke these words, which was funny to Penelope, since she had once been the most *pitying* of them all.

Tillie turned to Vicki and fixed her with a piercing stare. She spoke slowly and methodically, like their Fundamental Languages teacher when she conjugated verbs for the class. "If . . . I . . . wanted . . . pity . . . Vicki . . . I . . . wouldn't . . . come . . . to . . . you."

From Vicki's mouth came a sound that was half-chortle, half-sob: *"Bwah!"*

Stacy rushed to her defense. "You can't make us feel bad for you, Tillie."

"I don't think I could make you feel *anything,* Stacy," snapped Tillie. It was an able response on Tillie's part — at least Penelope thought so — but her voice wavered slightly, a sign to the circle to move in just a little bit closer. It reminded Penelope of an episode she'd seen of *Mutual of Omaha's Wild Kingdom* about what happens when packs of lions smell blood.

Penelope thought, *I am one of those lions.*

It was time, Annabella told them, to get to the point. "We don't care that you told Dr. Alvin," she told

Tillie. She paused as a crackling wind blew brittle bits of twig at Tillie's bare head.

"We care about the other stuff."

"What *other* stuff?"

"You know what you did, Tillie. You defamed us! You slandered us!" Annabella's mother was a libel attorney who specialized in cases of unfair character assassination, so she knew a lot of the lingo. "And the most pathetic thing is: You were one of us!"

"It's pitiful!" shouted Vicki, who'd gained strength from the circle's collective fury.

"I de-what?-ed you!" cried Tillie, who was having trouble hearing over the roaring wind — it looked like it was about to rain — "I sland-ed you?"

"What? You don't speak English now?" shouted Pia, who took on the role of Annabella's interpreter. "She's saying: We know what you did. You wrote on the walls."

As a confused Tillie grappled to process this information, the circle closed in even tighter.

Penelope thought, *If I stand where I'm standing, but don't move in any closer, does it count?*

"You think we're dumb, don't you?" hollered Pia. "You think you can write whatever you want wherever you want?"

"Say whatever you want wherever you want!" prodded Annabella.

The other girls formed a chorus, chanting these

words as a refrain: "Write whatever you want! Say whatever you want!"

Red blotches rose from the neckline of Tillie's sweater up to her nose. Her eyes shone with tears, and her lips — chapped and purple from the cold — shook. "I can say what I want whenever I want," she warbled. "It's my right."

It was as if her own words propelled her into action, and she sprang toward the circle of girls caging her, hurling her twiggy body into Lillian and Pia. But they gripped each other's hands and easily pushed her back in. She panted for breath, hands jammed in her pockets, eyes wild and scared, and waited for whatever was going to happen next.

Annabella reacted to the flash of violence with an eerie calm. "Well, Tillie," she said ominously, "if you can say whatever you want whenever you want, I can, too. And I can write whatever I want wherever I want."

And then, in an efficient burst of movement, Annabella — with the precision of a highly trained soldier — swiped an uncapped black Magic Marker from the sleeve of her light blue down jacket and sliced it across Tillie's wrist, leaving an oozy black gash of ink.

"Hey!" cried a stunned Tillie, grabbing her wrist protectively.

"Oops, sorry," cooed Annabella. "And that's permanent ink."

It was as if with the word "ink," Annabella had

shouted, "Ready, aim, fire!" From the sleeves of down jackets and peacoats came seven more markers primed for attack.

They pecked.

They speared.

They poked.

They jabbed.

"Stop!" shouted Tillie. "Ow!" she shrieked.

They made bruiselike splots, razor-thin slashes, jagged lines, leaky smears. In all different colors, on Tillie's neck and forehead, across her hands and wrists, on her camel-colored peacoat, on her yellow scarf.

Penelope thought, *If I take out a pen and poke at the air with it but don't actually touch her, does it count?*

"Please!" begged Tillie. She did a wobbly spin, her eyes grazing the faces of her attackers. From Annabella and Pia to Annie and Lillian to Vicki and Stacy to Penelope.

"Penelope," she whimpered. "You."

The five-minute bell rang, and as fast as the circle had gathered, it dissipated, flying in all directions across the bleached-out field. As Penelope's legs took her storming across the field, she remembered how Tillie made her feel there were things about herself she hadn't known before. She thought, *Maybe she knows I didn't mean it. Maybe she knows it wasn't really me.*

She hovered underneath the bleachers and watched Tillie limp across the field — like an oily stain slowly spreading on her mother's linen tablecloth. Tillie reached the wooden fence that separated the field from the cobblestone path. She wrapped her scarf around her neck and put the hood of her coat over her head, and Penelope figured she must be crying.

If I go over to her now, will that take away what I did? thought Penelope.

Someone else beat her to it. A small, dark figure ambled toward Tillie; at first Penelope didn't recognize who it was. But when she wiped her eyes — she was crying herself now — she realized. The figure — who was tenderly reaching toward Tillie to console her, who was taking her backpack from her and helping her over the fence — was none other than Cass. She led Tillie away from the field, down a crooked walkway Penelope had somehow never seen before, and out of sight. It was the first time Penelope had seen Cass on campus.

And then Penelope was crying in bursts so powerful, they made her run. She ran not toward Algebra class, but down the cobblestone path from Gritzfield Hall to the cluster of cottages that held Elston Prep's admissions office and guidance counselors. She entered a gray stone house with a red thatched roof that looked like the gingerbread houses Penelope always wanted to make at Christmas but that Mrs. Schwartzbaum called tacky.

She sped down a hall plastered with framed poster-sized pictures of Elston Prep in the snow, Elston Prep covered in fall leaves, Elston Prep in black and white circa 1946, when it was an all-boys school. It looked like a nice place to go to school, and for a moment Penelope forgot she went there.

She found her way to a bathroom. It was a small bathroom, not like the kind students used, with only two stalls and a lock on the door. She stared in the mirror above the sink at her flat hair and swelling eyes, at the cold sore that hung like a tiny clump of raw hamburger meat on the side of her mouth.

I could pull this off, she thought.

I could pull out my hair, she thought.

It made her feel strong, thinking these things.

Except her body got weak like rubber cement. Her knees were all gooey; she was going to fall down. She made it into the stall; her knees hit the hard tiled floor, her back scraped against the toilet, and her forehead banged into the door as it slapped toward her.

She pressed her chin into her kneecaps and cried, only it wasn't regular crying; it was long, hard wallops so big, they made her entire body shake, like someone was punching her from the inside. She grabbed her backpack and cried into that, hoping it would muffle the sound her wails made — like *The Love Boat* coming into harbor, like Stacy's cat Mitzi before she barfed. She cried until there was no cry left, until her chest sucked in and puffed out, and the loud wails became jagged breaths, like a donkey but slower:

Hee . . . haw.

Hee . . . haw.

Hee . . . haw.

She wanted to be little, she wanted to shrink. She wanted to be tiny like that family in a movie she once saw where the people were an inch high and slept in mouse holes, who used handkerchiefs as blankets, cereal bowls as swimming pools, tongue depressors as diving boards.

Or maybe she wanted to go back. She didn't want to be twelve. She didn't want to be in the seventh grade. She didn't want to think about college or Algebra or divorce or Fred Something or affairs. Yes, that's it. She wanted to go back! But what age would she be? Ten? Nine? Seven? Five? Maybe five. They all seemed too old.

Huddled in the corner of the unfamiliar bathroom stall, making donkey noises into a backpack, Penelope couldn't find an age that would make her as small as, at that very moment, she felt. She wanted to be so small, there was nothing left.

She had no idea how long she sat there, how long it was before the hammering of knocks on the door became full-on pounding.

"PENELOPE SCHWARTZBAUM, I KNOW YOU'RE IN THERE!"

Chapter Eighteen

Dr. Alvin had been the one to collect Penelope from the bathroom, and she'd taken her straight to Mr. Bobkin's office, where she got a stern talking-to about cutting classes. And to cut a class she was clearly struggling in, no less! Did Penelope realize, Mr. Bobkin wondered out loud, how very poorly she was faring in his Algebra class?

And then there was the matter of defacing school property, and Mr. Bobkin relayed how perfectly appalled he'd been to discover, written on the very desk where she sat, "Penelope B. Schwartzbaum Was Here."

"It's not the kind of thing you can blame on someone else," he bellowed, though blaming someone else hadn't crossed Penelope's mind. In fact, not much was crossing Penelope's mind.

Dr. Alvin had a more plain-faced approach. "Why did you deface the desk in Mr. Bobkin's room?" she inquired. Penelope told them she hadn't meant to, and Dr. Alvin asked what she could possibly mean by that. Penelope said she hadn't realized she was doing it when she did it, a response that so perplexed the literal-minded Dr. Alvin, she completely ignored it.

"Were you claiming your territory?" she asked.

Penelope had no idea what that meant.

"Were you marking your spot? That's what graffiti artists do, you know."

Penelope said she wasn't a graffiti artist.

"No, but you wrote your name where you're not supposed to. I'm not sure I know the difference."

Penelope didn't know what to say to that.

"Here's my question for you, young lady," puffed Mr. Bobkin. "What kind of statement were you trying to make?"

She wasn't trying to make any statement, she told him.

"The very act of vandalizing school property is a statement," he blasted.

They'd be discussing an appropriate punishment with the principal and the guidance counselor, Mr. Bobkin forewarned. They'd be calling her parents, Dr. Alvin added. She should go home, do her homework, and proceed as she normally would.

They'd let her know what was going to happen to her.

During the days that followed, Penelope felt like she was in a bubble. It was like the woozy feeling that had followed Penelope throughout the school year had finally captured her once and for all; it had swaddled her completely and now there was an invisible barrier between her and the world. She shook her head when she was supposed to; nodded when she was supposed to;

stared straight at the blackboard when she needed to; ran around the track in gym; watched *General Hospital*. But she did it all from inside a bubble.

She went to Bloomingdale's in the bubble. She still hadn't signed her new charge card. The woman ringing up her purple angora sweater dress wouldn't let her buy it without doing so. Penelope's pen hovered above the blank white band. Out of the corner of her eye she saw the salesperson's impatient fingertips drumming on the counter; and through the din of Bloomingdale's in-store music and the hum in her head, she heard a man behind her grumble, "Get a move on, kid, we don't have all day."

She allowed her pen to glide along the card's smooth surface, performing its ritual loops. There. It was done. Inside the bubble, decisions that had once been crucial seemed less so.

Penelope even attended Annabella's bat mitzvah in the bubble. She watched Annabella's lips move when she gave her speech, which had something to do with the prophet Jeremiah, the threat of nuclear war, and planting trees in Israel. She stood when she was supposed to stand. She bowed when she was supposed to bow. She faced east when she was supposed to face east, though she wasn't quite sure which way was east.

At the party, a glassblower sculpted miniature blue dolphins and crystal unicorns with a blowtorch.

Penelope drank three Shirley Temples. She danced to "The Time Warp" with Stacy and Vicki. She jumped to the left, took steps to the right, and screamed with everyone else: "It'll drive you insane-ane-ane-ane."

Penelope watched Annabella's uncles put her in a chair and lift her high above their balding heads as whooping guests wove vines around them. She watched Annabella's high heel hurdle through the air straight for Pia's forehead. She watched Annabella screech delightedly. She watched Pia cry in pain.

She saw Stacy in her new Gunne Sax dress, white eyelet with red trim, get asked to dance by Ben, who turned out to be Annabella's camp friend and therefore an acceptable new kid, the only one. She saw them dance a fast dance and then a slow one, then another fast one and another slow one. She saw Stacy whisper in his ear. She saw Ben give Stacy a crystal unicorn. She saw Stacy's mouth twist into a grin, the kind Penelope hadn't seen her make since the days when they hollered "West is best!" on the school bus, when scouring Broadway Nut Shop for new candy and collecting fortune cookies from Empire Szechuan were acceptable ways to pass the time.

For dessert, a woman dressed like Heidi passed out meringues shaped like mushrooms from a big wicker basket, and a man with a big chef's hat steered an enormous silver tray of strawberries dipped in chocolate. There was a cake, coconut white with ice blue frosting, in the shape of a giant cloud. When Annabella placed the knife on the icing, flashbulbs sparked, and her father raised a glass to toast: "May you always soar to new heights."

Penelope did all these things, saw all this happen. But were it not for the party favor — a T-shirt that said I WAS AT ANNABELLA'S BAT MITZVAH, 1982 — Penelope might not have remembered she'd been there.

Chapter Nineteen

If there was a price to pay for all the ignoring Penelope had done, she wondered if living in a bubble was it. She wondered if all the little tricks she'd done to *stop thinking* had backfired; they'd been too tiring for her brain. Now she'd have to live like this forever.

Would it be so bad?

Had anything *really* changed?

Nathaniel still sang; Jenny still played Elvis Costello; and Mrs. Schwartzbaum was still Mrs. Schwartzbaum: "Oh, Penelope, I got a call from your homeroom teacher — What's her name, Dr. Alvin? — if you see her at school tomorrow, can you tell her I'm sorry I didn't call her back? Fred and I were just so busy with our charity event. I'm sure it's just some field trip for your class she's calling about — right?"

In some ways, the bubble made life easier. Like on the day after Annabella's bat mitzvah, when Stacy called to ecstatically announce that she and Ben were the seventh grade's first official couple. Penelope hadn't needed to stop herself from thinking bad thoughts — if she even had them anymore.

"How come you never mentioned Ben was in your Algebra class?" asked an outraged Stacy. "He says you *won't* talk to him. He says you're mean to him!"

And when Penelope countered that she thought she wasn't *supposed* to talk to him, because he was new, because of The Pledge, Stacy seemed mystified. How could she not have known? Didn't she read the *No Newks Newsletter*? How could she not have heard? That there was one new boy who was okay? That it was Ben? Could Penelope really be *that* spacey? Could she really be *that* out of it? Just think — Stacy could have met Ben months ago if Penelope had been paying attention! If somewhere buried in Penelope there was a clever retort, she didn't think to look for it.

Shirley Commack picked up the other phone. "Oh hi, Penelope," she said. "I miss you. We never see you anymore." Then she asked Stacy to hang up so she could use the phone to call her editor.

That same afternoon, Mr. Schwartzbaum departed for Cairo by way of Amsterdam and Paris. Since planning the upcoming charity event was so time-consuming for Mrs. Schwartzbaum, and she needed to be at the office over the weekend, she hired Jenny to come on Sunday evening.

Penelope and Nathaniel played Boggle at the kitchen table while Jenny made dinner.

"'Erf' is not a word," Penelope told her brother.

"Jen-ny!" sang Nathaniel. "Is 'erf' a word?"

"Nathaniel, 'erf' is not a word," said Jenny. "Don't be silly."

He slumped in his chair and bitterly scratched "erf" from his word list.

"Think you kids can manage not to kill each other over a game while I run to the supermarket? I'm making lasagna, and we're out of tomato paste." Jenny slipped one arm into her pearly white ski jacket and then the other, and said she'd be back in a few minutes.

"If 'erf' is not a word, then neither is 'free,'" argued Nathaniel when Jenny closed the door to the apartment.

"But 'free' *is* a word," Penelope said, and sighed, putting a checkmark next to the word. She was winning twenty to one.

"'Free' is not a word, 'free' is not a word, I don't care, 'free' is not a word!" sang Nathaniel stupidly. He jumped up from the table and grabbed a head of garlic from the cutting board on the kitchen counter. He clutched it in his fist, waving his arms in the air in giant S-like swooshes.

"I hate Boggle. Let's play Space instead. Come on, Penelope! *Whirrrr . . . wizzzzzzz!* Look it's a spaceship! An alien spaceship!"

"You've been watching too much *Star Trek,*" said Penelope.

"It's USS *Garlic!*" whooped Nathaniel. "USS *Garlic* heading for Planet Garlic." He did his best imitation of a walkie-talkie. "Come in, Planet Garlic. Come in, Planet Garlic!

"Psssst, Penelope," he instructed. "You're supposed to say 'Come in' now. Say something like, 'I hear you, Planet Garlic.' Or, 'Loud and clear, Planet Garlic.'"

She ignored him.

"Come on, Penelope!" he shouted. "Play!"

He bounded over to her, arms swinging, dangling the garlic in front of her face. "I'm gonna hypnotize you into playing Planet Garlic!" He swung his fist back and forth like he'd seen hypnotists on cartoons do so many times before. "You are getting sleepy . . . sleepy . . . ," he gurgled. "You will play Planet Garlic with Nathaniel," droned her brother. "You will play. . . ."

And then Penelope did something peculiarly un-like her. She lifted her arm with a force she hadn't known she could muster, and propelled it forward as if to punch — except she grabbed Nathaniel's wrist instead. She squeezed as hard as she could until his silly, happy eyes started to water.

She squeezed until — squealing with pain — his fist unclenched and the head of garlic dropped to the floor. With her brother's eyes upon her, she held her foot above it — her once-gleaming-white Tretorn was now gray and scuffed and doodled upon — and brought her foot down with a brutal slam. Once, twice, three times, then four, stamping until the peel came undone and the head of garlic was no longer a head of garlic but lots of little cloves.

What was it that finally pushed Penelope to be so cruel? Was it the itch of the garlic's papery skin as it skimmed the tip of her nose? Was it the pungent stench that had clogged her nostrils? Was it Nathaniel's unrelenting will to play?

"Why'd you do that?" sobbed Nathaniel.

She didn't answer.

"Penelope? Why'd you crush my spaceship?" he choked, dropping to his knees and searching the floor for the scattered cloves. "Now the Martians will have no way to get to Planet Garlic," he snuffled.

On any other day, the sight of the little boy — gently scooping a smashed clove of garlic into the palm of his hand as if it were a wounded bird — might have made Penelope feel sad. Guilty, too. But if she felt anything, it was from inside the bubble. The violent thumps of her sneaker had done nothing to make it burst.

"Poor Martians," moaned Nathaniel, "now you're stuck here."

Penelope spent the rest of the night lying on her bed, staring at the ceiling, an activity interrupted only once — when the phone rang. She picked it up to hear a husky, faraway voice booming in the receiver: "Say what you mean!" blasted the voice.

"Hello?" gulped Penelope.

"Mean what you say!" the voice hollered.

"Who is this?"

"We know it was you!"

The voice repeated the sentence. Over and over again: "Say what you mean. Mean what you say. We know it was you." Penelope heard the click of a tape recorder and then Elvis Costello singing. *Was that Elvis Costello singing?* It was. "Didn't they teach you anything except how to be cruel in that charm school?" went the song.

If the callers had intended to talk, Penelope didn't give them the chance. Shaking, she hung up, and when the phone rang again, she didn't pick it up. "Let it ring! Don't pick up!" she called to Jenny and Nathaniel. "It's a wrong number!"

The next morning she and Nathaniel waited for the school bus. The lobby smelled like lemon furniture polish and percolated Spanish coffee, and Nathaniel curled up on the leather sofa in a gentle doze. Penelope sat uneasily beside him. She didn't have to be a detective to know the crank callers had been Tillie and Cass.

She considered not going to school, spending the day looking for Moes. Maybe she'd go upstairs, tell her mother she was sick.

She didn't even get that far.

It wasn't like Mrs. Schwartzbaum to call attention to family troubles in public — that was something she called tacky — but here she was in the middle of the lobby, wearing the Japanese robe and slippers Mr. Schwartzbaum had bought her in Tokyo.

"WELL, PENELOPE, GUESS WHO'S NOT GOING TO SCHOOL TODAY?"

Chapter Twenty

"Just a little bit wider, Pen, can ya?"

Penelope stretched her mouth open until her jaw felt like it would pop. Dr. Lincoln pressed a silver wand against the inside of her cheek. "This will feel a little icy. . . ."

Mrs. Schwartzbaum saw Penelope's week-long suspension from school as an opportunity to get some overdue dentist's appointments out of the way. Penelope needed several teeth pulled before she could get braces, and to Mrs. Schwartzbaum, minor oral surgery under general anesthesia seemed a fitting way for Penelope to see out her punishment.

"Good girl," said Dr. Lincoln. "Okay, so, you know that we're gonna have to put you out to do the extractions. You'll go to sleep for a bit. You might feel a bit hazy afterward, but trust me, it'll go away."

"Okay," said Penelope.

"Being put to sleep isn't pleasant, but it's better than being in pain."

Dr. Lincoln said he'd be back in a bit, and Penelope waited, lying on a big gray chair in a small, white, windowless room, staring at a poster of a little girl with a twinkly-toothed smile. The poster said: HAPPY TEETH MAKE HAPPY KIDS!

"I'm here to prep you for extractions," hummed Bonnie, the dental hygienist. "Penelope, I know it's a lot to ask, but do you think you could relax?"

"Sorry," said Penelope, trying to unclench her shoulder. It tensed more with Bonnie's touch.

"I don't think the person about to have oral surgery should be apologizing!" laughed Bonnie. She inserted two metal tubes into Penelope's mouth: one that sent cinnamon-scented water spurting against the inside of her back teeth, and another that sucked up Penelope's spit like a vacuum. It made a *shh shh* sound and tickled the bottom of her tongue.

She asked Penelope to bite down on a piece of canvas-covered plastic. It tasted like a combination of toothpaste, gas stations, and Barbie dolls. "Breathe out of your mouth, Penelope. Breathe into this." Bonnie placed a canvas mask in front of Penelope's face.

Soon she was asleep.

The last thing Penelope looked at before falling asleep was the poster of the girl, and the first thing she dreamed about were the girl's teeth. They weren't attached to the little girl any longer; they were floating in space, perfect and straight and white, against a black starless sky. There were hundreds of them. Tiny teeth whizzing in the darkness.

And then the teeth became Boggle cubes. Each one had a letter. And the letters spelled words.

PEN
CRUEL
NOBODY
IGNORE
STATEMENT
BUBBLE
MATCH
OPINION

Then all the cubes fell away until only one was left. O P I N I O N. The tiles bobbed up and down in the darkness like buoys, and then the P bobbed down and didn't bob up again. Then the I. Until what remained of the word O P I N I O N was O N I O N.

A word inside a word!

And then there were onions. All kinds. Miniature pearl onions. White onions. Yellow onions. Red ones. Pink ones. And Penelope's dream had gone from black and white to Technicolor. Now there was an entire solar system of vegetables: eggplants, potatoes, tomatoes, peppers, zucchini, carrot sticks and celery stalks and shining white heads of garlic.

And there Penelope was. *That was her, right?* She'd never seen herself from a distance before. She was balancing like a surfer on top of an orange pepper. The air felt velvety against her arms as she leaped onto the squishy head of a mushroom. She bounced from the mushroom to the eggplant to the tomato to the squash, playing a wild game of vegetable hopscotch. She went around and around, until it was time to lie down. She arched her back over a head of garlic, so the blood rushed to her head and her feet dangled in the air. The world was quiet, and nothing was moving except her wiggly bare toes.

When Penelope woke up, she was lying on a couch in one of Dr. Lincoln's waiting rooms. Her face was flat against a white cotton pillow, and a nubby blanket was stretched over her. She reached to touch her lips; they felt blubbery and numb, like they didn't belong to her. Her mouth tasted like salty cotton, and she reached inside to remove the blood-covered gauze scrunched against the gums where teeth had been.

She opened her eyes to discover Nathaniel staring straight at her.

"You're awake," he whispered. He'd been warned by Jenny to be as quiet as possible.

"Yeah."

"Do your teeth hurt?"

Penelope shook her head.

"Oh, well, that's good. You're lucky. Jenny says all you're gonna be able to eat is ice cream and you can get whatever kind you want."

Penelope nodded.

"Well, what kind are you gonna get? If she lets you get two, can one of them be Rocky Road?"

Penelope looked at her brother and wondered if maybe she was still dreaming. He looked different to her. Had he always had those freckles? Was his blond hair getting browner? As he pleaded the case for Rocky Road (It's three flavors, not just one!), Penelope thought, *I grow up, and so does he.* It was a simple thought, and it came out sounding like one of the weird haiku poems they studied in sixth-grade English class; but at that moment, to Penelope, it made all the sense in the world. She called to him. "Hey, Nathaniel!" She sucked in her breath, swallowing blood and gritty bits of gauze in the process. "You know where I was all this time? You know where I was?"

"The dentist?" answered Nathaniel hesitantly. He was still wondering about the Rocky Road.

Her mouth had filled with spit, and she swallowed a second time. "I was on Planet Garlic."

It hurt Penelope's mouth to smile, but Nathaniel's grin was contagious. "Ow," she moaned, though not unhappily. Maybe other people felt hazy after oral surgery, but Penelope felt more awake than she had for days. The bubble had popped.

Penelope's lips were still numb, which made it difficult to talk. "That doesn't matter," her mother snapped. "We'll do all the talking. That is" — she interrupted herself to send a searing look at Herbert Schwartzbaum across the table — "if your jetlagged father agrees to put down his puzzle."

Having been away, Herbert Schwartzbaum had lots of puzzles to catch up on.

"What were you *thinking* writing on a desk?" That was Mrs. Schwartzbaum, she'd had her face-to-face conference with Dr. Alvin while Penelope was at the dentist.

"I *wasn't* thinking," slurred Penelope.

"I should say not!"

"I-I blanked out."

"What do you mean blanked out? What kind of excuse is that, blanked out?"

Mr. Schwartzbaum's agitated foot tapping on the floor sounded like a machine gun going off. "Stop that, Herbert!" hissed Mrs. Schwartzbaum.

"Listen, Penelope, you're not going to get anywhere in life if you don't pay attention. You've got to be alert. From now on you're going to bed earlier. And you've got to modify your behavior. Writing on desks! Like a vandal! What's that about? Were you trying to be cool or something? You know, that's going to go on your permanent record. On your college transcript! You do know seventh grade counts for college, right? You better believe Dr. Alvin didn't hesitate to remind me of that."

Penelope touched a spoon of melted ice cream to her lips to see if she could feel the metal's coldness.

"Herbert, do you have anything to add?" demanded Mrs. Schwartzbaum.

Penelope's father tugged at his mustache. "Huh?"

"Well, I guess that answers that," huffed Mrs. Schwartzbaum. She told Penelope they'd be hiring her an Algebra tutor, and then she was off to attend a party with Fred Something and other luminaries from the worlds of art and finance, leaving Penelope and her father alone at the kitchen table with a puzzle of empty boxes and words that needed to go in them.

"I'm gonna go lie down," said Penelope unsteadily.

"Hey, kiddo," her father called to her, his eyes never straying from his puzzle. "Writing on furniture is a bad habit. Start doing that around here, and, well . . ." His mustache gave a mischievous twitch. "Well, we can only imagine how your mother would react then."

Penelope didn't know what to say.

"How about using something unorthodox? You know, like paper?" As if that reminded him of something, he reached inside his blazer pocket and pulled out a flat paper bag. He slid it along the table toward Penelope. "Sorry, I didn't have a chance to buy gifts this time."

Inside the bag was a folder of stationery from a hotel her father had stayed at in Amsterdam, a spiral notebook that said WELCOME TO HOLLAND on the front, and a gold pen stamped with THE RITZ: PARIS logo.

It was the first time he hadn't brought her back a doll.

Chapter Twenty-one

When Penelope stepped off the school bus after her suspension, she knew exactly what she had to do, and it didn't involve watching Vicki and Stacy sip coffee with half-and-half in the cafeteria.

Instead, she walked across the field. Her stomach fell as her feet treaded the very place where Tillie had been attacked. She bit her lip, still tender from the dentist, and followed the crooked walkway she'd seen Cass take. Penelope had never been to this part of campus before. Behind her a voice screamed, "Hey, man, wait up!" Another yelled: "Kaufman, do we have glee club now or what?" She kept going.

The crooked walkway became a set of steps. Penelope followed them down and found herself in front of The Elston Art Center. Inside, it wasn't as clean as Gritzfield Hall or as newly renovated as the Solden Science Center. The paint on the walls was peeling, and the hallways were lined with canvases in all different sizes. At the end of the hallway, off to the left, was a room called The Annex.

The door creaked open to reveal wood tables covered in blank pieces of paper and littered with charcoal pencils, rulers, and markers (markers!). There were older girls sipping Pepsi Light and listening to Walk-men. And there, in a corner, huddled over their Earth Science textbooks, were Cass and Tillie.

Penelope didn't even know how she'd known where to find them. So how come it seemed like they were expecting her? They looked at her at once, then stood up and grabbed their backpacks.

There is no chance, thought Penelope. *Say something,* she told herself. *Talk!*

Cass and Tillie had their backs to her now. She watched them walk away from her — was that still a bit of blue ink on Tillie's neck? was that the bumblebee shirt Cass was wearing? — and then Cass turned to Penelope and, with a flick of the wrist, motioned for her to follow.

I deserve whatever I get, thought Penelope, marching several steps behind them.

I'll take it.

Except all Cass and Tillie did was give her a tour. First, the girls' bathroom on the second floor of the Solden Science Center, then the girls' bathroom in the gym. Then Gritzfield Hall. It was a silent tour. They didn't want to talk; they just wanted to show her that the writing was gone.

Over the weekend and during Penelope's suspension, all of the bathrooms had been repainted. It had been part of a larger maintenance job, the repainting; the sinks had new faucets, chipped tiles had been replaced. But, regardless — whether the point was to remove the graffiti or not — the writing was gone. Penelope stared in awe at the bright white walls. *They look so clean,* she thought. *It's like nobody was here.*

The five-minute warning bell clanged as they emerged from Gritzfield Hall, and facing Cass and Tillie, standing in the cold, Penelope willed herself to speak. Out of her mouth flew a hundred embarrassed apologies, a thousand "I'm so sorry's." She couldn't find the words to say exactly what she felt, but Tillie and Cass seemed to understand. Somehow they knew that even if the words hadn't found their way out yet, they were somewhere inside Penelope. It was just a matter of time.

January turned to February, and Penelope spent the break between semesters watching Rick and Monica's affair fizzle on *General Hospital*, playing video games at Baronet with Nathaniel, looking for Moe Was Heres with Tillie and Cass, and studying Algebra with her tutor. She was a dorm mate of Jenny's, and sometimes after their sessions, she'd eat dinner with them, listening to Elvis Costello during dessert. Cass's favorite song was "Watching the Detectives," which was actually a violent song that had nothing to do with detectives, but she liked to pretend it did.

Every now and then, Penelope ate dinner at Empire Szechuan with Stacy and Shirley Commack. Ben even came along sometimes. Shirley Commack was wary of him until he told her he didn't believe in thinking about colleges until at least eleventh grade, and, anyway, he was thinking of joining the Peace Corps. Sometimes Penelope would meet Stacy and Ben at Baronet for video games. Ben loved the Upper West Side, and through his eyes Stacy learned to like it again, too — so Penelope had to figure that was a good thing.

Still, there were some afternoons when Penelope passed Stacy's apartment building and felt the strangeness of it all. To not even go up! To not even say hi to the doorman or Bernice! She'd force herself to keep going, then trip her way up Broadway, the immensity of loss churning in her belly, feeling like the world was tilted.

But then she'd think about her dream about the rope ladder. She'd see Stacy scaling the rope ladder; she'd see herself falling. She wasn't sure what it meant, if it meant anything at all. But she sure slept a lot better not having that dream anymore.

Life was easier not having the bad thought, too. Sometimes Penelope even let herself have a *new* thought: that she and Stacy might *match* again someday, that it was just a matter of time.

And, so, Stacy got closer to Vicki and, to Pia's dismay, to Annabella. Not long after Stacy met Ben, Annabella found a boyfriend, too, a new kid she met in her F. L. class. With their first kiss came the collapse of The

Pledge and the No Newks crusade. Dr. Alvin's threats became moot, The *No Newks Newksletter* ceased publication, and *No Newkers* traded their NO NEWKS T-shirts for college ones like the upperclassmen wore.

It was over, despite Pia Smith's desperate attempts to rally the troops, despite everything. Annabella had broken her own rules — or maybe it was more like the rules were changing. Or maybe that was just growing up.

Part Three

Chapter Twenty-two

"Duck!"

Penelope's kneecaps smacked the concrete. "Ow!" she managed to yelp before Cass's hand clamped her mouth shut.

"I on't chee zem? Dew ewe chee zem?" mumbled Penelope from behind Cass's hand.

"No, I don't see them," answered Cass, removing her hand and wiping her palm against the leg of her jeans. "Yuck! How many teeth did the dentist pull? I think I touched your gums."

"If you don't see them, why'd you tell me to duck?"

"It was a test. I was testing your reflexes."

"Yeah, well, I think you broke them," scowled Penelope; she massaged her throbbing kneecaps.

"At least we know we're in the right place." Cass pointed to the folding chairs arranged in neat rows along the sandbox.

Penelope and Cass hadn't been invited to the launch party for the East Village Community Playground, but that hadn't stopped them from attending. In fact, they'd walked seventeen blocks and taken two buses and one cab to get there.

The playground had been designed by artists represented by Fred Something with funding from

Mrs. Schwartzbaum's bank. "Boy, are these kids lucky!" Penelope's mother had exclaimed that morning. "Do you think they know they'll be sliding their little bottoms down an Yves de la Veaux? Climbing a Theo Buckley jungle gym?"

Indeed, this was the charity function that Penelope's mother had been "toiling on day in and day out." She'd come home gleeful when a famous artist agreed to participate, disgruntled when a famous socialite declined to RSVP. She was hoping for a gigantic turnout — and also to get some coverage on the local news. "We'll reel them in with famous folk," she explained, "but this is really about the children."

Mrs. Schwartzbaum was so excited about the event, she was having her hair colored and her makeup professionally done — just in case she got on the news. And if she didn't, "Well, what the heck! It's not often you get to enjoy the fruits of your labor!"

For Penelope and Cass, attending the party had an obvious appeal as well: They got to see Mrs. Schwartzbaum and Fred Something in action. Plus, Kip Harwood, the artist Cass had suspected of being the Upper West Side's most notorious graffiti artist Moe, had painted a mural on the playground wall. It was covered with a white sheet, today would be the unveiling, and he would be there. So perhaps they'd finally get to see Moe!

Penelope and Cass were scrunched behind the water fountain, peering out at the activity. A crowd was forming, but Penelope's mother and Fred Something were yet to arrive. "I sure am glad Bea's not married," said Cass out of nowhere.

"Why, so you don't have to worry about her having an affair with someone?" asked Penelope, scanning the crowd.

"Yeah, and just 'cause it's dumb."

"What's dumb?"

"Marriage."

"Why?"

"Weddings, women wearing white dresses, vows — I don't get it. It doesn't make sense to me."

"How can it not make sense to you? Everyone does it."

"So, everyone does Algebra, and it doesn't make sense to you."

"Hey!" gulped Penelope, who didn't need to be reminded of her mathematical shortcomings.

"I know some people just think it comes naturally. Grow up, get old, get married. But I think it sounds dumb. Throw some big party just because people decide to live together? I want to live with Sylvia Hempel for the rest of my life. Did anyone throw a party for us?"

"Your parents were married," Penelope argued. "You don't think they're dumb."

"Well, who knows?" said Cass. "If their car hadn't crashed, they might be divorced by now." Sometimes Cass Levin said very disturbing things.

By the time Tillie joined them, a large crowd had formed. Small children from the neighborhood fidgeted in folding chairs, and artists with dyed blue hair, wearing paint-splattered T-shirts and neon pink sweatpants, mingled with bankers in wide suits and skinny ties.

Fred Something had finally arrived. Penelope first spotted him standing alongside a man with braided hair in a banana-colored jumpsuit. They were in front of the white sheet covering the mural, doing an interview with Eyewitness News.

"Do you think that's Moe?" Cass asked.

Penelope craned her neck to get a better look at the man in the yellow suit, but blocking her view was a frizzy head she actually recognized — it belonged to Shirley Commack, who was taking notes in one of her reporter notebooks.

Stacy's mom was here, but hers wasn't? Where was Mrs. Schwartzbaum?

"Maybe she had to go into the office," offered Tillie.

"Or maybe she's just late," suggested Cass. But just as the word "late" left Cass's lips, a choral group launched into a song about "letting the children play," and the charity event began. Four six-year-old kids read a poem about art. And Fred Something said some words about the merging of form and function.

The grand finale was the unveiling of Kip Harwood's mural. Kip Harwood was, in fact, the man in the yellow suit, and he seemed quite pleased with his picture, which featured one-eyed neon green aliens with shovels and buckets playing in a sandbox of magenta sand. The minute she saw it, Penelope knew there was no way he could be Moe. Moe wouldn't paint kids as aliens. He'd make a much better statement than that.

After the unveiling, the little kids broke in the new playground, and artists and bankers sipped red wine. Penelope watched Shirley Commack scurry from artist to artist doing interviews. She seemed to like doing her job, and Penelope felt a flash of missing her.

The crowd started to thin and Mrs. Schwartzbaum still hadn't shown. Still, when Fred Something left, the girls decided to follow him.

Penelope, Tillie, and Cass walked a careful ten steps behind Fred Something. He ambled west on Fourteenth Street, past stores advertising T-shirts for a dollar and jeans for five. On Seventh Avenue, he bought the *New York Times* at a newsstand, then ducked into a subway station.

"I've never taken the subway alone!" gulped Tillie as they fought their way underground. Neither had Penelope or Cass.

The subway was faster than the bus, that was for sure. The girls hovered around a silver pole, several seats away from Fred Something, who was reading the newspaper.

"If he sees us, we'll just say we're coming from a field trip for school," instructed Cass.

"Where should we say we went?"

"The zoo."

"The zoo's uptown and east."

"A museum, then."

They were trying to think of a museum downtown, when Fred Something folded his paper and put it in the side pocket of his camel-colored blazer. He combed his hair with the fingers of his left hand, checked for lint on his lapel, and got off at the next stop. They followed him.

In the middle of Seventy-second Street between Broadway and West End, Fred Something stopped so abruptly, the girls skidded in their sneakers to stop short. Penelope collided with Cass, who slid into Tillie, who was so nervous about getting caught, she froze in a position that reminded Penelope of the mime with the white-painted face who performed on the corner of Fifty-ninth Street and Central Park South.

"This isn't freeze-tag, Tillie!" Cass said, and laughed, collecting herself. Except none of them could move as they watched Fred Something give his blazer one more brush with his hands and walk down the steps of a tiny restaurant called the All State Café. Music from a juke-box blasted onto the street when he opened the door. This did not look like a place Mrs. Schwartzbaum would go!

The girls ducked into a deli next door. "I don't think we can go in there," said Cass. "It looks very small. He'll see us for sure."

"Yeah," said Tillie. "And I think we'd stand out. It doesn't look like there'd be anyone our age in there."

They weren't sure what to do next. Then, through the deli's glass doors, Penelope spied a familiar figure strolling diagonally across Seventy-second Street.

It was Jenny.

Jenny's blond hair, particularly sleek this evening, looked like velvet theater curtains opening and closing around her face as she walked. She wore a fuzzy yellow sweater over white Levi's and pink clogs.

"Where's she going?" asked Cass.

Penelope exited the deli and called out to Jenny, but the honk of a bus obscured her voice and before Penelope could yell again, Jenny disappeared — down the stairs and into the All State Café.

The All State Café!

Where Fred Something was!

Well, this was sure going to be something, thought Penelope. If Jenny saw Fred Something and her mother dining together at the All State Café, what would she say? She was probably meeting the girls from her dorm, and wouldn't that be weird to see Fred Something and Mrs. Schwartzbaum! Would she figure it out?

They bided their time in the deli, but Cass said just being around food — it was almost dinnertime now — was making her hungry. They moved on to the stationery store, where they took turns being the lookout person.

There were many close calls.

"I think that's her!"

"Ooops, sorry, that just looks like her."

"Here she comes!"

"Sorry. My mistake."

"Penelope, isn't that your mom?"

"Oh, gosh, sorry, that's a man."

"There! There!"

"Sorry. I'm so hungry, I'm hallucinating."

A half hour into their second stakeout of the day, and Mrs. Schwartzbaum hadn't shown — again. Cass decided it was time to make a move. Maybe they'd missed Penelope's mother. Maybe she'd already been *in* the All State Café when Fred Something got there. She decided that Tillie — having met neither Fred Something nor Jenny — should scope it out.

Tillie wasn't crazy about this idea, but Cass said there were no other options. "C'mon, it's this or failure." She gave Tillie explicit instructions: "It's a three-step process. Number one. Ask to use the bathroom. Number two. Pay close attention to the person Fred

Something's with. Number three. Leave. Think you can handle it?"

"But what if they don't let me use the bathroom?" Tillie asked nervously. Out of habit, she reached to pull at a clump of hair, caught herself, and jammed her hands in her jeans' pocket instead.

"Improvise!" commanded Cass, who must have been very hungry. She wasn't a very violent person, but she practically shoved Tillie down the stairs.

Chapter Twenty-three

"He's with her!" yelped Tillie when, five long minutes later, she emerged from the All State Café. She flailed her arms. "He's with her!"

"Who's her?" begged Cass. "Why are you jumping? Who? Penelope's mom?"

"No," Tillie cried excitedly, shaking her head wildly. "With the girl walking across the street! The blond one!"

"Fred Something is with Jenny?" gasped Cass.

"Jenny's with Fred Something?" gasped Penelope.

Tillie nodded.

"No way."

"Yes way."

"No."

"Yes."

"Uh-uh."

"Ah-hah."

They went on like this for a while.

"And get this?" shouted Tillie, clearly pleased to be playing such a crucial role in the escapade. "They were kissing! Kiss-ing! A *kiss* kiss! On the lips and every-thing!" Tillie sang. "That happened before I went to the bathroom. And then, when I came back, they were holding hands!"

"I'm going to faint!" whooped Cass, looking *not at all* like someone who was going to faint.

"Me, too!" shrieked Penelope, who was actually feeling a bit woozy.

"It was really gross," said Tillie.

"What? The kiss? The kiss was gross?" Cass and Penelope looked on at their friend in horror. They could only imagine what was involved with a gross kiss. Spit? Tongues?

"No, the bathroom," Tillie said, and laughed. "The kiss looked" — she paused thoughtfully — "the kiss looked nice."

Once Cass and Penelope were convinced that the kiss was a couples-kind-of-kiss, that Jenny and Fred were on a date, and that the "age-inappropriate paramour" Bea had heard about was *NOT* Mrs. Schwartzbaum but Jenny — *Jenny! Jenny!* — they linked their arms to create a chain and spun in circles.

Out of their mouths came brassy hoots and gleeful snorts. They laughed until their voices cracked and their bodies trembled. The stationery store owner accused them of being public nuisances, and an old man in a Yankees windbreaker thwacked Penelope in the shin with his umbrella.

The sky was a dark shade of lavender, and they hadn't even noticed it was raining out. They sprinted to the Utopia Coffee Shop, where they ordered grilled cheese sandwiches on rye, onion rings to share, and three Cokes.

After dinner, Cass and Tillie decided to walk Penelope home, then share a cab across town. It was drizzling now, and Penelope and Cass crossed Broadway holding a plastic bag over their heads. Tillie said she liked the way the rain felt on her short haircut, which sprouted from her head in tiny wet spikes.

West End Avenue looked bigger when it was dark and windy out; yet, tonight, it still managed to make Penelope feel snug. On Seventy-seventh Street, they hit a red light. Waiting at the curb, the rain falling harder now, Penelope turned her gaze down the block toward Riverside Park.

The street was empty except for a solitary shadowy figure standing in front of a red brownstone; he appeared to be a hunched man poking at the sidewalk with a stick. At first Penelope thought the stick was a metal detector, but then a car stopped, and for a brief moment the yellow headlights illuminated the street, and Penelope realized the stick wasn't a metal detector but a cane, and the man, small and soggy in his plastic rain poncho, wasn't poking at the sidewalk, he was writing.

He was writing.

She tiptoed several steps closer, careful not to make sloshing noises in the puddles.

"Hello!" she hollered.

There was no answer.

"Hello?"

There was no response.

The car was gone, and without the help of headlights, Penelope had to squint. She screamed to the man one more time. Nothing. He simply wagged his cane in the air, turned to face Riverside Drive, and hobbled off. He was a slow, unsturdy man, yet Penelope — who was so transfixed she needed several minutes to collect herself — had the eerie sensation that he'd evaporated before her eyes. She didn't have to look at the square of sidewalk he'd abandoned to know it said:

MOE WAS HERE.

Penelope kept standing there. Voices came from behind her.

"He didn't *look* crazy," she heard Tillie say.

"Why are we standing here? We should go catch up to him," she heard Cass say.

But none of them made a move. The wind grew gusty, and they resumed their walk uptown.

"Who'd have thought Moe would turn out to be a hundred!" exclaimed Cass, finally. They were a block away from Penelope's house. "Did you see the guy? He could barely walk."

"Or hear," added Tillie. "You were screaming loud, Penelope."

"He must really want to write his name in the street," marveled Cass. "To hobble around like that!"

"Well, maybe that's the only way he can make a statement," said Penelope. They were in front her house now. The night doorman, Jim, emerged to help Cass and Tillie hail a cab.

Chapter Twenty-four

What happened to Mrs. Schwartzbaum on the day of the big charity event? To figure it out, Penelope had to piece together bits of information culled from conversations she'd overheard.

It went something like this:

On the morning of the East Village Community Playground event, Jenny called the apartment. Mrs. Schwartzbaum was having her hair blown dry, so Mr. Schwartzbaum — who'd only just returned from a five-day stint in Brazil — took the call. Jenny said she'd received a dinner invitation from Fred Something, and she didn't want to put Penelope's mother in an awkward position by dating one of her clients. She also didn't want to jeopardize her job as Penelope and Nathaniel's mother's helper.

Mr. Schwartzbaum assured Jenny that going on a dinner date with Fred Whatever-his-name-is would be no problem, but thanked her for asking, then told her to have a good time. Penelope had to imagine he was doing a crossword puzzle while having the conversation.

Then Mrs. Schwartzbaum emerged from the bathroom, learned about the call, and instantaneously contracted a variety of ailments: her head was pounding, her stomach was aching, she had chills. All signs pointed to food poisoning from a spoiled wedge of Jarlsberg cheese she'd eaten the night before, and she got into bed, where she remained the entire weekend.

Then things began to change. Mrs. Schwartzbaum started coming home before dinnertime, ordering take-out with Penelope and Nathaniel, letting Jenny go home early. She stopped getting her hair done so often, claiming it was getting damaged from so many color treatments. For now, she said, she'd have to do with a little less luster.

And she stopped talking to Jenny about the fabulous functions she'd attended with the who's who of the art world, and spoke to her with the same clipped formality she used with the housekeeper. If Jenny noticed, she was too polite to mention it.

When Penelope and Nathaniel asked their mother if she was okay, she said yes, just tired, it had been a hard day. Did they have any idea what a grind her job was? She was so tired. She promised them that next year, it would be different. She was going to make a change. No more overtime. No more business dinners. She was going to set limits.

She never mentioned Fred Something anymore, but Penelope knew her mother had to miss him. If she'd learned anything this year, it was that there were words inside words — there were *whole worlds* inside words! — and Mrs. Schwartzbaum might be saying one thing, but she meant something else. She may not have had an affair, but she'd given Fred Something her heart, as Carlos would say, and even Penelope, who'd never had a boyfriend, knew that was a big deal.

Some days Penelope would look at her mother and feel sorry for everything. She'd feel sorry for the stray cats in the North Shore Animal League commercials on TV, she'd feel sorry for the foreign dolls her father had given her that were collecting dust on her shelves. She'd feel sorry for the peanut butter congealing at the bottom of the jar, for Nathaniel's Matchbox car that had lost its wheel, for the empty squares in her father's crossword puzzle.

She even felt sorry for the Sunburst Clock when Mrs. Schwartzbaum decided that it no longer went with the décor and needed to come down.

The pleasure of

your company is requested

at the home of

Bea and Cass Levin

for a

FonDon't Party

May 1, 1982

8:00 p.m.

Please arrive hungry.

Performances encouraged.

R.S.V.P. to Sylvia Hempel.

Chapter Twenty-five

"Welcome to your first FonDon't party!" shouted Bea Levin from the window of the little yellow townhouse. "I'll be right down to let you in."

Bea and Cass lived on a quiet street on the East Side, a few blocks up from Bloomingdale's. They lived on the top three floors of the four-story building and rented the downstairs apartment to artists from out of town. "Come in, come in. I'm so sorry your parents couldn't make it!" Bea opened the door and swept Penelope and Nathaniel inside. The foyer smelled like dried flowers and Sylvia Hempel.

"So, can I trust you two to be honest about something?" Bea gave them a serious look. "Cass says I look like a bat in this outfit."

She was wearing a shiny black top made of a papery fabric with the hugest sleeves Penelope had ever seen. The sleeves were triangular, and they hung to Bea's waist. Holding them outstretched, they looked like wings.

"It looks like origami," said Penelope, because it was the first thing to pop into her head. She hoped it wasn't an insult.

Bea lowered her arms and beamed at Penelope. "You're an observant girl, Penelope, perceptive. As a matter of fact, a Japanese designer friend gave this to me. I'm on *the edge* of the cutting edge of fashion and all Cass can say is that I look like a bitey little creature from the zoo."

"I like bats," chirped Nathaniel.

Bea's wrinkly face lit up. "Well, I like your outfit, too, Nathaniel!" she clapped. "But I should have told your parents not to dress you up. This is a FonDon't party. Get it? Fondue? Fon do? Fon don't? FonDon't. Oh, well, you will."

Penelope had never seen a room with more colors than Bea Levin's living room. And patterns, too. There was a pink armchair with tiny green dragonflies, a green silk couch spotted with red-and-yellow-checked pillows, a fuzzy orange rug specked with maroon. And stacked on coffee tables and lying on the floor were books upon books upon books. They had oil paintings and photographs for covers and were the biggest, heaviest books Penelope had ever seen.

Her eyes zigzagged every which way, and it took her a second to notice a gargantuan woman lounging on a deep purple chaise. She had long, stringy hair, black except for a big white skunk streak down the middle. She was reading under a yellow lamp, which gave her large, pale cheeks a pumpkiny hue.

"Doris, these are Cass's friends, Penelope and Nathaniel."

Doris looked up from her book; she blinked

drowsily like a cat waking up. "Oh, I'm sorry. I was just so absorbed. Penelope, Nathaniel, hi, I've heard so much about you." She had a soothing voice, and Penelope wondered if she took a lot of cough syrup.

"Doris is Cass's aunt," said Bea.

"I'm Cass's father's sister," explained Doris.

"I thought Cass's father was dead," blurted Nathaniel. Penelope kicked him in the back of the knee. "Ow," he yelped.

"Don't worry. Dead isn't a bad word," Doris told them. "And, yes, dear, he is dead. But I'm still his sister. I always will be. Funny how it works that way." She looked importantly at Penelope and Nathaniel, and Penelope didn't know what to feel first: uneasy under the large woman's gaze, or guilty for kicking Nathaniel.

"Hey, hi, hi, hey! No one told me you were here! How come no one told me you were here?" yelled Cass as she bounded down the stairs, shaggy Sylvia Hempel clicking at her heels.

"Well, if you weren't listening to that music at a zillion decibels, you would have heard them arrive yourself, Cass. I'm surprised you haven't damaged your eardrums. Not to mention poor Sylvia Hempel's."

Cass looked sheepishly at Bea, then turned to Penelope. "Guess what? Doris went to London and brought me back every Elvis Costello! You gotta hear 'em!"

"How about you give these poor thirsty children a

drink before you squirrel them away in your bedroom. I got all the ingredients you asked for. Meanwhile, Doris and I will work on the FonDon't's."

Bea had bought the ingredients for Purple Cows, which they slurped from yellow glasses. Cass gave Nathaniel his in a mug shaped like Snoopy's nose.

Soon, the rest of the guests arrived. Tillie was first. Over spring vacation, she'd gone to an allergist who prescribed a new cream that seemed to be working. She had only the slightest trace of a rash remaining, and it was on the backs of her knees. The doctor said it was a temporary reaction to the medicine. Only Tillie, they laughed, could be allergic to allergy medicine.

Next were Doris's friends, two long-haired men who wore rings on their fingers and played Bulgarian folk music at a bar up by Columbia University. One carried a guitar, and the other, two oddly shaped drums that looked straight out of a Dr. Seuss book.

The last to arrive were the biggest surprise: Jenny and Fred Something. Fred Something wore a boxy white suit over a red button-down shirt; Jenny wore a blue-and-white striped oxford, a gauzy yellow skirt, white beaded sandals, and a pink coral necklace. It was similar to something Annabella Blumberg would wear. *But Jenny looks a lot better,* Penelope thought proudly.

Fred Something handed Bea a bouquet of large-toothed tropical flowers called birds-of-paradise. He had a gift for Cass, too, a comic book he'd picked up in

Paris. She'd end up giving it to Nathaniel, but everyone thought it was nice of Fred Something to remember there were two hostesses.

Dinner was set in the sculpture garden. The trees were strung with Christmas lights, and Bea lit thick cream-colored candles that smelled like Ivory soap to keep away the bugs. They sat on a thick red blanket around a wooden picnic table — only it was really only a picnic table top, because it didn't have legs, only stumps. There was room enough to sit under it if you took off your shoes and crossed your legs.

Laid out on the table were lidded crocks full of mysterious concoctions and baskets covered in black velvet napkins, the contents of which would be revealed once everyone was seated and toasts were made.

On Bea's request, Nathaniel had changed into an old purple T-shirt of Cass's. Bea hadn't wanted to send him home with a mucked-up shirt, and he seemed much happier without the tight collar Mrs. Schwartzbaum had forced him into. Looking at her little brother next to Jenny across the table, Penelope thought about how jolting seeing the most familiar faces in unexpected settings could be, and how this wasn't jolting at all. She thought: *I feel more at home than at home*.

Bea clinked a wineglass with her fingernail and welcomed everyone to the table. "Cass, would you like to do the honors?"

Cass rose. She then explained the origins of the

FonDon't party. "My parents, Bess and Will, loved fondue," she told the crowd. "They loved it so much, they wanted to eat it all the time. Except I thought it was stinky." She wrinkled her nose at the memory. "I still do. Anyway, they started to do this ritual. They'd make fondue for themselves, and they'd make another fondue for me — only mine wasn't really fondue, because it rarely had cheese in it. That's why we call it FonDon't." She motioned to the table of crocks. "You'll see for yourself in a sec.

"When my parents died, FonDon't was all I wanted to eat. I moved in with Bea." Cass looked to Bea as she said this; Bea raised her glass a little higher. "And she said we could eat FonDon't as much as I wanted. She even helped me come up with new recipes. Doris would come over and lots of different people and we made a party of it. Now it's like a holiday — the kind that comes whenever you want it to, whenever you need it to. Just" — Cass paused a moment to sip from her water glass — "whenever we want to celebrate my parents. . . ."

Cass turned out to be a very effective public speaker. When she was done, Bea asked that everyone raise their glasses to toast Bess and Will Levin, "who had open minds and open hearts, and who knew that there was no one single recipe for living in this world."

"FonDon't!" screamed the folk musicians.

"FonDon't!" screamed everybody else.

Doris was next. "Bess and Will explored the world outside, but what they cared about most was the world within. We — all of us here — are capable of so much. Inside us are sloping countrysides, bustling cities, hot days and snowstorms, beauty, ugliness, greatness. It's all in there — no matter how small we may sometimes feel, no matter how small we may still be." She smiled at Nathaniel when she said this last line and raised her glass. "May every day be full to bursting."

"FonDon't!"

Penelope tilted a crystal flute to her lips and drank the pear cider Tillie had brought Bea as a gift from her mother; it bubbled in her mouth, sweet and bitter all at once.

With the majesty of a court magician, Cass uncovered the first FonDon't: a crock of melted American cheese accompanied by a basket of buttery bits of toast. When you dipped the toast in the cheese, it tasted like the grilled cheese sandwich from the Utopia Coffee Shop.

There was the Texas FonDon't, which was meat chili swirling with cheddar cheese. It came with a basket of French fries sprinkled with cayenne pepper.

There was the Indian FonDon't, which Doris had invented after a trip to Bombay. She wouldn't reveal the ingredients. All she'd say was that yogurt and mangoes were involved. She'd even baked a special Indian bread, thick and white and flecked with pepper and herbs.

They used skewers, not forks, and speared and dipped until the crocks were nearly empty, at which point they switched to fingers and hands. They skimmed their thumbs along the insides of the crocks and sucked on their fingers.

To raging applause, the guitarist stuck his entire face in the Popeye FonDon't (melted mozzarella and spinach). And somehow Tillie ended up with peanut butter and jelly FonDon't in her ear.

"I . . . don't . . . think . . . I . . . will . . . ever . . . eat . . . again," moaned Tillie.

"Tell me about it," whimpered Penelope.

"Bet you guys ten dollars you will!" Cass said, laughing. "Wait till you see dessert. It's not a FonDon't party if you don't have dessert."

Lucky for Penelope and Tillie, Bea required that they take a break between courses, and the party moved into the living room. Penelope, Cass, and Tillie lay on their backs in the middle of the orange rug. "How are you girls going to digest that way?" laughed Doris, sinking into an armchair with a grunt.

The folk musicians played music that sounded like weird twangs to Penelope, but the adults seemed impressed. When the drummer did a solo on his Dr. Seuss drum, Doris jumped to the floor and wiggled her large body like a wet grizzly bear shaking itself dry.

"They're okay, but this is no Elvis C," whispered Cass so only Penelope could hear.

"I know who's next!" Bea shouted when the set ended. "I'm not sure if everyone knows this, but we have a musical prodigy in the house. The next Cole Porter, if you will."

She looked to Nathaniel, who stood up with uncharacteristic shyness. Cass's T-shirt, streaked with FonDon't, draped to his knees, making him look particularly small.

"This is about a place I'd like to go," he announced "I made it up myself."

"If I can hear a clock tick
That means I know where I'm not
I'm not where I wanna be
'Cause there are no clocks on Planet Garlic
No hours or minutes or alarms that go off
No school and no place we have to be
Only you and me
But there are no clocks on Planet Garlic
There are dogs and cats and little Martians, too
They look like kangaroos
We can go to Planet Squash if you say so
Jenny says it's on the way, so
All we have to do is a magic trick
But I'd like to stay on Planet Garlic."

There was a moment of silence after Nathaniel's final trill, and then the room erupted in roaring

Bravissimos. Fred Something and Jenny rose to their feet, holding cigarette lighters in the air, apparently something people did at rock concerts.

"Planet Garlic, you get a guitar lick!" roared the guitarist, and he played a riff in Nathaniel's honor.

"That was great, but what does it mean?" Tillie whispered in Penelope's ear.

"I guess you could say it's a private joke," Penelope whispered back. She didn't think she'd ever felt this proud.

Fred Something was next to stand up. He coughed twice, glanced over at Jenny, who gave him an encouraging smile, then said: "I'm not a performer, but I do have an announcement." He coughed again. "Thanks to the generosity of a certain sculpture collector, and with a loan from some generous and hopefully not foolhardy financiers, I'm starting my own art gallery in London."

There was applause.

"Thanks, but that's not really the good news." He scratched at his chin and studied the carpet for a moment. "The good news is I've asked Jenny to come with me. And" — he coughed again — "she's agreed." He grinned a zany kind of grin Penelope thought only children were capable of. Then he said: "We're moving to England."

The musicians played a jig that sounded more Irish

than English, but no one cared. Bea and Doris scrambled for the nearest bottle of champagne. All the clattering and commotion brought Sylvia Hempel running into the room, barking to the drumbeat, batting down glasses with her wagging tail.

Penelope didn't know what this meant. Jenny was moving to England? For the summer? Forever? She glanced at Nathaniel huddled in the oversized big T-shirt. He was caught up in the frenzy, laughing with Jenny — how could he help it? — and Penelope saw he didn't understand what perhaps had just happened: that Jenny's good news might very well be bad news for them.

She'd have to break it to him later — or maybe she wouldn't — maybe she'd just be there when he figured it out for himself.

Cass hadn't been joking about dessert. There was a whole new set of FonDon't crocks. They dipped apple slices into hot melted caramel for Caramel Apple Fon-Don't, marshmallows into melted Hershey bars for Hot Chocolate FonDon't, and butter cookies into hot raspberry sauce for Fruity FonDon't.

Tillie's mouth was full of Fruity FonDon't when Bea asked her how her mom was doing. Tillie struggled to swallow, but the words still sounded garbled: "She says that for the first time in a long time, she feels unstuck."

To Cass and Penelope, the last word was completely

indecipherable. "Unstunk? Untucked?" they asked. Tillie had taken a bite of butter cookie and stared at them, while chewing.

"Unstuck, you goofs." Doris laughed, coming to Tillie's rescue. "Like she's not stuck anymore."

"I still don't get what it means," said Cass in her usual blunt manner.

"According to my mom," Tillie explained, "it's like seeing the world from a whole new angle." Cass said that sounded cool, then proceeded to load her mouth with marshmallows, washing them down with a hefty gulp of the melted chocolate crock.

"Unstuck is *very* cool indeed," said Bea, sending a kind smile Tillie's way. "You must be very proud." Tillie was, and to prove it she chugalugged straight from the crock of raspberry sauce.

Penelope watched her friends laughing, and gobbling food and knew exactly how Cherry Warner felt. If she'd thought she'd never been this full in her life *before* dessert, she was wrong. She'd gone from full to bursting.

Chapter Twenty-six

Finals arrived, and Penelope didn't know how it had happened. When had February turned to March to April to May? Seventh grade had started slow, but it sure was ending fast. Soon it would be June, and she'd be trading her faded Levi's for Dolphin racing shorts, her tube socks for Peds — and she was hoping for the kind that had pom-poms.

With Bea Levin's seal of approval — despite her association with Fred Something, it still carried weight — Mr. and Mrs. Schwartzbaum enrolled Penelope at the same camp Cass was attending. "It's a beautiful place in Vermont," boasted Bea Levin, "for artists. They teach writing and painting and filmmaking."

When Penelope protested that she wasn't an artist Bea waved her off: "Somehow I don't think it'll take much to find an artist in you, Penelope," she said. She tried to sell Cherry Warner on the camp as well. That way the three girls could spend the summer together. But Cherry and Tillie were taking a road trip — just the two of them — starting in New York City and heading who-knew-where. "You can't be more unstuck than that!" praised Bea.

The night before Tillie left, she, Cass, and Penelope

had a slumber party. They had Penthouse C to themselves, as Mr. and Mrs. Schwartzbaum were attending a gallery opening in SoHo. They were leaving the girls in charge of Nathaniel — good preparation, Mrs. Schwartzbaum reminded Penelope, for next year, when she and her brother would be on their own after school.

As it turned out, Jenny would be their last mother's helper ever. Mrs. Schwartzbaum acted like she was rewarding Penelope when she dubbed her "old enough to take care of Nathaniel." The truth was that Jenny was moving to London for good, and had given her resignation to Mrs. Schwartzbaum. Penelope thought, *It's not that I'm old enough to take care of Nathaniel, it's that I want to*. She was pretty sure there was a difference.

On Tillie's last night, they ate pizza while watching television, listened to Elvis Costello, and, when it was time, put Nathaniel to bed. The girls took turns reading to Nathaniel from the book *Charlotte's Web*. Tillie read: "'There in the center of the web, neatly woven in block letters, was a message. It said: SOME PIG! Lurvy felt weak. He brushed his hand across his eyes and stared harder at Charlotte's web. . . .'"

Cass leaned over to Penelope and whispered, "See, Charlotte was a graffiti artist, too."

♥♥♥♥♥

They made sleeping bags of blankets and went to sleep on the floor of Penelope's room, which was half-packed, half-not. Mrs. Schwartzbaum had offered to have it redone over the summer, which made Penelope think back to Stacy's room, with its rainbow sheets and empty shelves. She decided against it, but asked if she could make some room by storing stuff she didn't use, like her foreign doll collection.

Snug in the blankets, Tillie, Penelope, and Cass talked about all sorts of subjects — like where Tillie would go on her trip, whether Cass and Penelope would be bunk mates at camp, and if Fred Something and Jenny would eventually get married.

Cass, of course, said she sure hoped not.

"What if Bea gets married? You're not going to be happy for her?" asked Tillie.

"That's not going to happen."

"But what if it does?" Tillie had gotten used to Cass's confident declarations and liked to challenge them.

"If it does, I'll be happy for her. Bea says it's okay to question tradition, but I still have to accept people who embrace it."

"I just hope my mom doesn't get married again soon," Tillie said. "She *just started* to get happy."

Tillie and Cass fell asleep before Penelope. They breathed so differently — Cass in deep *hmmms*, Tillie

215

in soft asthmatic snores — it was like listening to two different radio stations playing at once. Penelope found it difficult to fall asleep herself.

Her tossing woke Cass. "What's happening?" she murmured. Penelope explained, and Cass suggested they try to breathe together. She counted down:

3

2

1

Breathe!

But keeping the same pace was very difficult. They'd get it right for a few breaths, and then Cass would cough or Penelope would sniffle or they'd hear Tillie wheeze, and they'd have to start over again.

It turned out breathing at the same pace with someone was impossible, and Penelope suddenly felt very bad for married people who slept in the same bed every night. Would Jenny and Fred Something be able to breathe together? Could her parents?

Penelope looked over to Cass. She'd fallen back to sleep, and a tiny puddle of drool had formed on her pillow. It was funny that somebody with so many ideas in her head, so many opinions, could sleep so soundly. Sometimes Penelope wondered if, by making this new friend who thought *so many things,* she'd simply traded one set of opinions for another. That was a scary thought, a *bad thought, even,* but she had to let herself think it from time to time.

Penelope had been wrong about so many things, and she wondered if maybe she was thinking about breathing wrong, too. Maybe it was this: There were all sorts of people in the world, and maybe it wasn't about *breathing together* or *matching,* maybe it was about learning *not to breathe together* and learning *not to match.*

Wondering about this, she fell fast asleep.

Lookout Mountain Camp for the Arts looked very different from Elston Prep, with its rolling hills and clapboard houses. Penelope and Cass lived in a cabin painted toothpaste green. They spent their days rowing boats, swimming in the lake, doing ceramics and macramé. Penelope signed up for a cooking course and a calligraphy course; Cass took short story writing; and two nights a week they watched old black-and-white movies in the camp's dining hall.

Tillie sent postcards from strange places like Tucson, Arizona, and Palm Springs, California; Nathaniel mailed tapes of songs he'd written and performed, including a duet with Bea and Sylvia Hempel; and Jenny sent pictures of herself and Fred Something in front of London tourist spots like Buckingham Palace and Big Ben.

June turned to July. Cass finished four short stories, and Penelope created a recipe for Purple Cow FonDon't. And when July turned to August, they started talking about going home and what eighth grade at Elston Prep would be like, whether Geometry would be harder than Algebra, and whether Penelope should get clear or metal braces.

The air, gnatty and steamy when they arrived, was clear and cool now; and soon came their final day at camp. Bea was having a FonDon't party the night of their return. The Schwartzbaums would be coming; Tillie and Cherry, too. So, as sad as Cass and Penelope were to leave, they were excited to get home.

On their last morning they stripped their beds, packed their trunks, and ate one final breakfast in the dining hall. They said good-bye to their bunk mates and their counselors, promising to return next year. And when Cass dashed off to make one last purchase at the camp canteen, Penelope said a private good-bye to their cabin. She wanted to give it something to remember her by. She already had a spot picked out.

She removed a blue felt-tip calligraphy pen from her jeans shorts pocket, and on the wall above the bed where she'd slept all summer, she wrote:

Somebody was here.

She could have written more, but that was all she had to say. Anyway, she had to go. Cass was waiting.

THINK SEVENTH GRADE WAS TOUGH?
DON'T MISS THE NEXT EXCITING TALE
FROM ELSTON PREP:

The Pity Party

8th Grade in the Life of Me, Cass

HERE'S A SNEAK PEEK. . . .

... from *The Pity Party*

All Cass's life, her favorite subject was English. But with one glance at the reading list for Ms. Glitch's fourth-period class, she knew that was about to change. Every single book was about an orphan. *Oliver Twist*, *Huckleberry Finn*, *Jane Eyre*. Orphan, orphan, orphan! What kind of sicko assigns a million books about orphans?

Cass was mulling this over, when suddenly everyone in the classroom was talking at once. Cass turned her attention away from the reading list and toward the commotion.

Here was something Cass had observed: You could tell a lot about a person based on how she entered a room. Some people (like Penelope) shrunk when they entered a room, but others (like Bea) made a room shrink when they entered it. On the first day of school, most students skidded into class, fidgety and squirrel-eyed: "Am I in the right place? Is this English class?" But Annabella Blumberg, the eighth grade's most popular girl, simply glided in.

Cass wasn't obsessed with Annabella — at least not in the way everyone else was. She didn't care about how pretty Annabella was or what clothes she wore. She definitely didn't want to be friends with her, but she did like watching her — in the way scientists on nature shows observe their subjects, anonymously and from a safe distance.

Annabella didn't look around to see who else was in the class, or double-check her schedule, or even catch a glimpse of the teacher. She sauntered over to a desk and slunk into a chair, as if to say that any place she ended up was the right place to be.

TO PENELOPE
(Open When Bored)
I wish for my sake you were in my English class, but I'm glad for your sake you're not.

#1. This teacher might be psycho.

#2. Guess who's in this class: Yup, LILLIAN LANG, and . . . .

#3. ANNABELLA DUMB BERG (Yes, I know, I'm immature!)

Ms. Glitch had a burbly way of speaking, as if her voice was coming from inside an aquarium instead of the front of a classroom. "Levine, Cass? Are you here? Cass Levine, hello?"

Considering the dread she'd invoked in Cass, Ms. Glitch was a surprisingly puny woman. Cass coughed loudly — as if a frog in her throat was what had delayed her response. "Yes, I'm here," she told the teacher, "but it's Levin. Cass. Levin." Cass hadn't meant to sound haughty, but she wasn't upset that she did.

"Oh dear, my mistake," warbled Ms. Glitch apologetically, scribbling a correction in her notebook. "Okay, who's next, let's see. . . . Ah, we have a new student. Punkin, Rod? Rod Punkin? Please say I have that right."

The response came from directly behind Cass. "Positively presently present is Punkin, Rod!" barked a boy with the rat-a-tat precision of a machine gun.

There was tittering in the room. "I'll interpret that as 'Here,'" said Ms. Glitch after it died down.

Cass whipped her head around. A crazy grin gawked back. Rod Punkin was a spiky-headed boy in a striped T-shirt unraveling at the neck. On his desk, facing her, was a piece of loose-leaf paper propped up like a triangle.

HEY, LEVIN NOT LEVINE, WANT TO GO
DOWN THE HILL WITH ME? MAYBE WE CAN
GET DUMB BURGERS. ROD

Next to the word "burger," he'd drawn a picture of a cheeseburger wearing a dunce cap. Cass turned back to face the teacher, her head exploding with all the horrible things "Go down the hill with me" might mean. She clapped her notebook shut, then, for extra protection, propped her elbows on top of it.

"Now, I know we've got a lot to cover this year," Ms. Glitch was saying, "dangling participles, thesis sentences, split infinitives. . . . But that doesn't mean we can't have fun." At the word "fun," Ms. Glitch picked up a copy of the reading list that drooped in the dull afternoon air. "On this reading list are some of my absolute all-time favorite books."

Some of your favorite books ABOUT ORPHANS, Cass thought crossly. *What DOES "go down the hill" mean?*

"We're going to read them. We're going to write about them. We're going to talk about them. And that brings me to the first order of the day." Ms. Glitch sunk to her knees to open a desk drawer, from which she pulled a large hat. The act reminded Cass of a bad magician who tries to pull a rabbit from a hat but gets only air. "In this hat are numbered pieces of paper," she announced mysteriously. "The number indicates which discussion group you're in." The room crackled with confused murmurs. "That's right, discussion groups. There are four students per group. You'll meet every Friday. I want you to see this as an opportunity."

"I want you to see this as my socks-are-hurting-me," said Rod Punkin in a whisper loud enough for only Cass to hear.

"You might think it odd at first," Ms. Glitch warned them. "All I ask is that you try to be open-minded."

"You might think this Rod's the worst. All I ask is you try not to be blinded."

Cass opened her notebook and scrawled another note to Penelope, this time in extra-gigantic letters, so that someone peeking from behind could see the words loud and clear.

REMIND ME TO TELL YOU ABOUT
THE KID WHO SITS BEHIND ME IN
ENGLISH CLASS. HE'S A FIRST-RATE
WORLD-CLASS PSYCHO!!!! WE'RE TALK-
ING SERIOUS BEHAVIOR PROBLEMS.

Ms. Glitch lay the hat on Lillian Lang's desk. Lillian acted like picking first was a privilege bestowed upon her, rather than a simple consequence of having chosen the first desk in the first row of the classroom. She made a big to-do of rolling up the sleeve of her oxford and showing off a wrist of bangles and woven friendship bracelets. *She probably made those for herself*, thought Cass. Lillian dipped two fingers, claw-like, into the hat, and rummaged around until Ms. Glitch reprimanded her: "Ms. Lang, we don't have all day."

"Mine says #1!" Lillian announced — as if that, too, signified greater meaning.

Cass picked briskly, but also got #1. *Please don't mean what I think this means,* she thought.

"This is your chance to get intimate with the material. . . ." The word "intimate" sent a current of snickers across the room. "Okay, okay," Ms. Glitch sighed, "bad choice of words. But that just goes to show you how important choosing your words can be. You'll keep that in mind when putting together your presentations."

"Presentations?"

"What's a presentation?"

It was a well-established fact at Elston Prep that discipline and rigor were the tickets to an Ivy League college, and so unstructured assignments were a source of great panic.

"Are we going to be graded?"

"You know, eighth grade marks count for college!"

Ms. Glitch took the hysteria in stride. "Each discussion group will make a presentation to the class," she explained calmly. "This presentation can take any form — a group skit, a song, you can act out a scene from a book in mime, as far as I'm concerned. Just as long as you're creative, just as long as you work together. We'll be starting with *Oliver Twist* by Charles Dickens, and I see no reason why the first group to present shouldn't be #1. Who's in #1?"

Two hands in front of Cass went up — one belonged to Lillian, of course; the other — Cass noticed with a gulp — to Annabella Blumberg. But where was the fourth? She turned her head to the right, the left. . . .

"Okay," said Ms. Glitch, making notations in her roll book. "#1 is Lang, Blumberg, Levin *not* Levine." She glanced at Cass and threw her a wink. "And, who's that in the back? Ah, yes, the inimitable Mr. Punkin."

It turned out being #1 was nothing short of doomed!

ALISON POLLET grew up on Manhattan's Upper West Side and attended a school similar to Elston Prep. Like Penelope, she often spaced out. Now Alison lives in Brooklyn, New York.